CORGI CASE FILES

CASE OF THE
HIGHLAND
HOUSE
HAUNTING

I0584056

J.M. POOLE

True happiness is being owned by a corgi!

Mysteries by J.M. Poole
The Corgi Case Files Series
Available in e-book and paperback

If you enjoy Epic Fantasy,
check out Jeff's other series:
Pirates of Perz
Tales of Lentari
Bakkian Chronicles

CORGI CASE FILES

Case of the
Highland
House
Haunting

Book 7

J.M. Poole

Secret Staircase Books

Case of the Highland House Haunting
Published by Secret Staircase Books, an imprint of
Columbine Publishing Group, LLC
PO Box 416, Angel Fire, NM 87710

Book layout and design by Secret Staircase Books
Cover images by Yevgen Kachurin, Irisangel, Felipe de Barros

First Secret Staircase paperback edition: January 2021
First Secret Staircase e-book edition: January 2021
* * *

Publisher's Cataloging-in-Publication Data

Poole, J.M.
Case of the Highland House Haunting / by J.M. Poole.
p. cm.
ISBN 978-1649140319 (paperback)
ISBN 978-1649140326 (e-book)

1. Zachary Anderson (Fictitious character)--Fiction. 2. Pomme
Valley, Oregon (fictitious location)—Fiction. 3. Haunted house
stories—Fiction. 4. Amateur sleuth—Fiction. 5. Pet detectives—
Fiction. I. Title

Corgi Case Files Mystery Series : Book 7.
Poole, J.M., Corgi Case Files mysteries.

BISAC : FICTION / Mystery & Detective.
813/.54

Giliane —

At the risk of sounding like a broken record, I wanted to tell you, again, that I count myself the luckiest man in the world to have you by my side each and every day.

Love you always & forever!

Acknowledgments

I never consider the publication of a book an achievement I earned by myself. There are a number of people I need to thank for their help. First up is my wife. I've said it before, and I'll say it again. Giliane is the hardest worker I have ever known. How she squeezes out enough time each day to do the things she has to do is beyond me. You have my eternal thanks, babe.

Up next would be the members of my Posse who helped me out this time around. We have Jason, Carol, Clare, Elizabeth, Louise, Caryl, Mefe, and Diane. You guys and gals have all added some polish to the book, and for that, I am (always!) eternally grateful.

The cover was once more illustrated by the multi-talented Felipe de Barros, an artist I found a while ago on DeviantArt.com. I know I've started quite a few emails to him that say, "Well, what do you think about…" I know it must be annoying. Felipe, fantastic work, amigo. Thanks again!

The last person I need to thank is… drum roll, please… you! Thank you very much for continuing to support an indie author. Your constant stream of emails, words of encouragement on Facebook, and the comments on my webpage make my day every single time.

Thank you. J.

PROLOGUE

And we're walking. We're walking. We've got a lot of places to see, so please try to keep up, okay? Timothy, where's your buddy? Go find him, please. And Terrence? Where's yours? Okay, we're coming to a stop. Now, what is the first ... kids? We're stopping. That means stop walking. Now, who can tell me what was the single most important rule of today's field trip? Anyone?"

"Stay together!" thirty kids chorused.

The teacher held a hand to her ear and pretended to be hard of hearing.

"I'm sorry, I didn't hear you. What was that?"

"STAY TOGETHER!" thirty voices screamed.

Acting supremely unaffected by the eardrum shattering response, the lead teacher smiled. She signaled to her partner, who was bringing up the rear of the group, and together, they began to walk. The first teacher gestured at an approaching house.

"Precisely. Now, boys and girls, what I want you to remember, as we're passing these lovely homes, is that many of them were built way back when your grandparents were no older than you are now."

"No way!" one boy exclaimed.

"Take this one, for example," the second teacher said, as the group came to a halt in front of a quaint Victorian story-and-a-half cottage. "This house is even older than your grandparents. It says here it was built in 1901. Who can tell me how old this house is?"

Not one child spoke.

"Come on, kids," the teacher scolded. "Math is one of the most useful subjects you'll ever use. Now, what year is it?"

"2019!" nearly half the students shouted.

"And if you subtract 1901 from 2019, what should we get?" the second teacher continued.

"Ermm, a hundred?" one boy hesitantly asked.

"You're close, Daniel," the first teacher said. "But, I think you'll find that it's a little older than that. Anyone else?"

"118 years," a quiet female voice all but whispered.

Both teachers zeroed in on the young girl who had answered and enthusiastically began applauding. The bespectacled 8-year-old girl in question blushed furiously and tried to hide behind her fellow students.

"Well done, Jennifer!" the first teacher praised. "You

are exactly correct. This house is 118 years old. Just think what it must have been like to live back then. William McKinley was President of the United States. And, do you know what was really fascinating? Steam-powered cars were more prolific than gasoline powered cars."

"Steam powered?" several kids repeated, confused.

"Steam and electric were more popular than gasoline," the first teacher added knowingly. "Does anyone know when the first gasoline-powered combustion engine vehicle was invented?"

There was another collective round of silence.

"I know what to do the next time I need them to be quiet," the second teacher quietly mumbled, eliciting a soft chuckle from the first.

First Teacher laughed and waved a dismissive hand, "Oh, don't worry. I wouldn't expect any of you to know that."

"When was it?" one boy curiously asked.

"1885," Second Teacher proudly answered. "I'll bet none of you know how much groceries cost back then."

"I doubt any of them do now," the first teacher muttered, under her breath.

Being careful to maintain a straight face, the second teacher continued.

"A gallon of milk was only fourteen cents, a five pound sack of flour went for twelve cents, and can anyone guess how much a pound of chocolate retailed for?"

"Ten dollars!" one boy shouted.

"Fifteen!" another added.

The second teacher smiled patronizingly at the group of students before singling out the one girl who had managed to get an answer right.

"Jennifer? What's your guess?"

"Umm, I'd say around thirty-four cents?"

The teacher's jaw dropped. Both teachers stared, dumbfounded, at the girl. How in the world could she have known that?

"Once more, you're exactly right!" First Teacher praised.

"Show-off," a few of the students muttered.

"I have to ask," Second Teacher hesitantly began, "how you could possibly have known that? I didn't know it until I read it from my notes here."

Jennifer shyly held up her phone. "Because I looked it up when you weren't looking."

The kids broke out in laughter as the two teachers flushed with embarrassment.

"Okay, that's one for you, Jennifer. Now, please put your phone away for the remainder of this excursion."

"Yes, ma'am."

The group walked on, coming to the next house on their list of places to see.

"Here we have one of Pomme Valley's finest treasures!" First Teacher crowed excitedly. "Highland House. It's a wonderful example of a Victorian Italianate villa. And, believe it or not, it's actually a little bit older than the last house."

"I want to go in," one voice said, belonging to a tousle-headed blonde boy.

First Teacher shook her head. "I'm afraid not. Do you see the construction trucks parked just outside? I do believe someone has finally bought this house and, from the looks of things, is renovating it."

"Wouldn't that be nice?" Second Teacher observed. "I

would love to see this one fully restored."

"But I wanna go in there!" the blonde boy repeated. "My daddy says it's haunted! I wanna see the ghost!"

An eleven-year-old boy hesitantly raised a hand.

"Please," First Teacher quietly scoffed. She quickly looked around and noticed all the kids were staring at her. "There's no such thing as ghosts. Now, if you would all look at ... yes, Steven?"

"You believe it's a haunted house, dontcha? Ain't ghosts been sighted in there before?"

"That isn't a word, Steven," the teacher firmly told the boy. "And to answer your question, there's no proof. I mean, there's no *reliable* confirmation that the lovely Highland House is frequented by ghosts."

Another boy raised a hand.

"Yes, Charles?"

"My sister went in there a couple of years ago. With her boyfriend. They said they encountered the ghost up on the second floor. Isn't it true that a ghost stays behind because of unfinished business?"

"And I thought I watched too many movies," Second Teacher softly groaned.

Sensing a chance to steer the conversation away from the supposed supernatural occurrences thought to exist in the two- story villa, First Teacher retrieved her own notes from her purse and began to read.

"Constructed in 1892, Highland House was built by Major General Harrison Highland, a veteran of the Spanish-American War. He settled here in the area, where he married a local girl in the late 1880s. They had one daughter, Miss Hilda Highland. A confirmed bachelorette, she was known to dabble in..."

First Teacher trailed off as a loud scream suddenly ripped through the air. The two adults fell silent as Highland House suddenly exploded with activity. Contractors were seen rushing out of the house, as though the Devil himself were chasing them. One man, wearing an orange hard hat and a bright yellow vest, caught sight of their group and rushed over.

"Do any of you have a phone?"

Both teachers nodded and immediately dug into their purses.

"Please call for an ambulance. Hurry! One of our guys has been electrocuted!"

ONE

"This has got to be the cutest little car ever! I mean, there are two seats, perfect for the two of us. Plus, there are six tires, for ... hmm. Why *are* there six tires?"

"It's for going over some rough terrain," I explained, as I navigated the utility vehicle over the worn dirt road.

"Can it go through water?" my passenger asked.

"It's not a boat," I clarified. "But, the guy that sold it to me said he's gone through some pretty deep puddles with it. Just for the record, no. I really don't plan on taking it through any water. Not unless I have to. If there are huge puddles around here, then we've got bigger problems to deal with."

Jillian Cooper laughed delightedly as I stepped on the gas. The 6x4 John Deere Gator may have only had a top speed of 20 mph, but when you're going over uneven terrain, it certainly felt a lot faster.

"May I drive it?"

I grinned and took my foot off the gas. After a few moments, the Gator came to a stop. I hopped out of the driver's seat and held out my hand.

"Sure! I mean, this may look like a big toy, and I'll admit that it *feels* like a big toy, but it really is a useful tool around here, especially when Lentari Cellars added all that additional land."

Well, let's go ahead and get the formalities out of the way. My name is Zachary Anderson, but my friends call me Zack. Sitting next to me here is my girlfriend, Jillian Cooper. And if you couldn't tell what we were doing, we were currently driving the winery's newest addition, the 6x4 Gator, around the property. I should also mention that I own my very own winery, *Lentari Cellars*. It's located off the Rascal River in southwestern Oregon, in a little town called Pomme Valley. If you were to look for us on a map, I can tell you that PV (as the locals call it) sits comfortably between two other towns, Grants Pass and Medford.

When I'm not purchasing large new toys, er, *tools* for the winery, I'm typically found indoors, in front of a computer. The other title I hold, and I've held it considerably longer than that of winery owner, is romance author. Yeah, yeah, I know what you're thinking. Not many male authors can say they're successful in the romance genre. Then again, I should also point out that all my readers believe I'm a woman.

For the record, in writer's lingo, it's called a pseudonym. Or a nom de plume. What's my nom de plume? *Chastity Wadsworth*. Don't laugh. That name sells books, and lots of 'em.

Oh, I should also mention that I hold a third title, and it's one that started last year. I'm a police consultant, but to be totally honest, I'm just a handler. Who does the PVPD really want to help solve a case? It certainly isn't me. You see, that distinction belongs to my dogs.

Sherlock and Watson are two of the smartest dogs I have ever encountered in my life. Sherlock chose me the moment I locked eyes on him in the pound after I moved here. As for Watson, well, I can thank a good friend for giving her to me.

Yes, Watson is a she.

I probably should've named her something different, only it went with Sherlock, who was already named when I broke him out of jail. Plus, they are about as unintimidating as you can possibly imagine. No, they aren't Rottweilers, or Pit Bulls, or anything like that. They're corgis. Pembroke Welsh Corgis, if you want to be exact.

While not the most popular breed of dog on the planet, I will say that they are probably the most adorable breed of dog you'll ever encounter. True, I *may* be biased. Then again, I've always said that the corgis are a big dog wrapped up in a small dog package. They're intelligent, loyal, and for some odd reason, my two dogs are the absolute best at solving murders.

I said, no laughing.

Sherlock and Watson have solved a number of cases now, and that includes, I'm sorry to say, a number of murders. Somehow, and I have no idea how, they always seem to be able to find clues pertinent to our case. As for me? I'm manual labor. I hold the leashes, provide their Royal Canineships with kibble, pick up their poo, and act like I know what I'm doing. But, in all reality, it's the dogs who are the celebrities.

Now, where were we? Ah, yes. Jillian and I were out touring the winery in our new (for us) Gator. I had just pulled over and was getting ready to explain the controls when Jillian stomped on the gas and the Gator took off like a shot. Fields were whizzing by us, one after the other. All had row after row of vines with big fat bunches of grapes, I couldn't help but proudly notice. Since this was the time of year where we were well into the ripening stage for the vines, practically every plant we passed had 2-3 clusters of big, fat grapes. In case you're wondering, yes, the vines were capable of producing more clusters than that, but we (meaning my winemaster, Caden) purposefully trimmed the clusters back so the vine could devote its energy into ripening just the clusters that were left. Think of it like pruning a rose bush. If you let too many flowers grow, then the poor plant overtaxes itself as it tries to keep all those blooms happy.

I don't know. I don't really understand it, either. Caden was the one who came up with that analogy. He's already proven to me that he knows what he's doing, so if he says we have to prune the vines, then so be it.

Jillian and I had just crested a small hill and were about to cross over into the winery's most recent acquisition of land when I felt the Gator slow.

"What's all this?" Jillian asked, with wonder evident in her voice. We drifted to a stop as Jillian waited for an answer.

I should explain.

We were looking at row after row of young trees. Not saplings, mind you, which would have suggested that no one here knew how to look at a calendar. This certainly wasn't the time to plant new trees, but I had been convinced to shell out even more money for older trees. I smiled and nodded as I looked at Caden's latest project. My winemaster had been hard at work, that's for sure. He and the rest of his team had said that the shipment had arrived and were eager to get them all planted. Looks like they were able to do it, all in less than a week.

"Those are fruit trees," I explained. "That section over there is apple trees, while the area to your right are the cherry trees."

"You've planted an orchard? How wonderful!"

"It's something Caden wants to try."

"And those over there?" Jillian asked, as she turned to point to a third section, directly behind the cherry trees. "Those don't really look like trees."

"An astute observation, Lady Cooper," I drawled, trying my best to sound like an English gentleman. "They are, indeed, not fruit trees, but fruit bushes."

Jillian giggled and swatted my arm.

"Stop talking like that, you silly man. You said this is Caden's idea? Does he want to open up a fruit stand?"

"That's what I thought he wanted to do, too," I confessed. "Then he explained what he had in mind. It never dawned on me that wine could be made by using fruits other than grapes."

Jillian excitedly clapped her hands together.

"Oh! I should have seen that coming! He's going to expand Lentari Cellar's offerings, isn't he?"

I nodded. "Yep. He admitted it'll take a while. These are more long-term plans, since I was told that the wine an apple produces typically has to be aged for at least two years."

"That is a long time," Jillian admitted.

"What are your favorites?" I asked. "Besides your fancy champagne, that is."

Crystal Rose was Jillian's favorite drink. To say that the woman had expensive tastes would be an understatement, as each bottle carried a $400 price tag. Before you ask, yes, I can confirm that's how much they cost since I have purchased a few bottles for her. More than a few, if you must know. Thankfully, Jillian doesn't drink it too often. Usually, it's to celebrate the holidays, or some personal achievement that either of us makes. To give you an example, I bought her a bottle when I announced my latest book had actually hit the *USA Today* best seller's list. While impressive, I had been shooting for the *NY Times*, but then again, beggars can't be choosers. For the record, I have hit both of the lists before, but it has been quite a while for either of them.

"Well, let's see," Jillian began, as she considered the question. "You obviously know about Crystal Rose. Do you know what I would suggest Lentari Cellars should try making? Berry wines. I've had a few that were fantastic. There's this winery in Salem that has several offerings, including gooseberry and elderberry."

I couldn't help it. I grinned. Then, I turned to point at the third section, namely the straight-as-an-arrow rows of young bushes.

"I'm really glad you said that. I know Caden has planted a variety over there, but some of the berries I do remember are marionberry, gooseberry, and blueberry."

"You like marionberries?" Jillian suddenly asked, interested. "They're one of my favorite berries."

"Lady, they *are* my favorite berry."

Jillian giggled and nodded appreciatively. "You guys are

really planning for the future, aren't you?"

"Caden is, I'm not. I just write the checks."

"If you don't mind me asking, where are you going to store all this new wine you two are going to make? You mentioned that much of the fruit-based wine requires several years to age."

"Funny you should mention that," I began, as I pointed at the large, distant building to the south. "The main winery building does have a few storerooms, but you're right. There's not much room there. If we're going to store barrels of wine, then we're going to need something a little bit bigger."

"We?" Jillian repeated, offering me a dazzling smile.

I looked at my girlfriend and slowly nodded. "Yeah, you heard right. That wasn't a pronoun problem. I value your opinion and like to think of the winery as ours."

Jillian leaned over and gave me a tender hug.

"Thank you, Zachary."

"You're welcome. So, speaking of storage, where do you think I should have the new warehouse built?"

"Hmm? You're going to build a new warehouse?"

I grinned. "Hey, I'm trying to think about the future, right? If this new venture takes off, and I have a feeling that it will as long as Caden is at the helm, then we're going to need a bigger place to allow the wine to age properly. With that being said, where do you think it ought to go?"

Jillian immediately turned and pointed back toward the winery.

"I'd say right next to the winery itself. There's a decent section of land on the east side of the building. That's more than enough room to make yourself a new storage facility."

"Isn't that where the students park their cars?" I asked.

"For Caden's classes? Probably. But, those kids are resourceful. There's still plenty of open land around there where they could park. It shouldn't be a problem for you. Or for him, for that matter."

I gave Jillian a warm smile and placed my hand over hers.

"Thanks. I appreciate the insight."

"You're welcome. And, for the record, I enjoy being included, even though you know you don't have to. So, as long as we're talking about expansions…"

"Are you looking to expand your cookbook store?" I asked, after Jillian trailed off.

"No, not that. Cookbook Nook is performing just fine. For a specialty book store here in PV, it has exceeded my expectations."

"If it ain't broke, don't fix it," I told her.

She nodded. "Exactly."

"Then, what'd you have in mind?"

"Are you familiar with any of the historic houses here in PV?"

"Only yours," I told her, as we resumed our tour of the newly planted orchard. "Carnation Cottage, right?"

"Yes. Well, there are a number of them located throughout PV. Have you heard about Highland House?"

I shrugged. "I've heard the name in passing a few times. I don't think I could tell you where it is. What about it?"

"Well, you may or may not have heard, but it has been purchased. By me. I'm going to turn it into a B&B."

"A bed and breakfast? Nice! Umm, don't you have enough to do with your book store?"

Jillian nodded. "I do, which is why I won't be running it. I have an old friend moving back into town who has tons of hotel management experience. I've already talked to her, and she says she's more than willing to run it for me."

"That seems awful convenient. You want to start another business, and have a friend who happens to have the skillset necessary to make it succeed. I'm curious. And please, if it feels like I'm pressuring you to divulge information I don't need to know, just say so."

"I think I know what you're going to ask, but I assure you, it is okay. Ask away."

I gave her a warm smile.

"Thanks. All right, what came first? The purchase of the property, or the phone call with your friend?"

Jillian smiled and nodded. "My phone call with Lisa. It just so happened that I learned Highland House was on the market earlier that same day."

I shrugged. "Okay. It must have been her lucky day."

Jillian shrugged. "I, er, have the financial abilities to help my friends out, as you know, and I'm always looking for a good investment. Highland House hadn't been on the market that long, less than a week, I believe. I've loved that house ever since I first laid eyes on it. So, as soon as I saw the For Sale sign, I contacted the realtor and told them I was interested. We negotiated a good price and voila!"

"One instant B&B," I murmured. "Wow, when you want to do something, you just get right out there and do it, don't you?"

"If you're worrying about my financial well-being," Jillian began, "then I can assure you that you don't have to. Michael was a very savvy businessman. He made sure that if anything ever happened to him, then I'd be taken care of."

Referencing her late husband always brought a pang of loss to Jillian's lovely face. The pain of losing a loved one never truly goes away. At best, the pain will become more bearable and you will learn to cope with it. I should know. I lost my wife to a car crash and her loss is something I still think about every single day. But, will I dwell on it? Does it control my every waking moment? No. As for Jillian, well, Michael, unfortunately, died from cancer several years ago. I never got a chance to know him, since I hadn't moved to PV just yet, but something tells me we would have gotten along just fine.

"How many businesses do you actually own here in PV?" I asked, genuinely curious. Then, with a shudder, I had one of my rare out-of-body experiences and heard how that must have sounded. "Sorry. I shouldn't be asking you those kinds of questions. It's none of my business."

Jillian drove to the side of the winery and parked next to the old flatbed truck, donated by Caden's father a few months back. She placed a reassuring hand over mine.

"Don't worry about it, Zachary. I ordinarily wouldn't confide this to anyone, but you're special. Quite honestly, I have more money than I know what to do with. I have been helping friends of mine start their businesses for a while now. Do I know how many? The answer is no, I don't. I have no idea how many businesses I either own or have a financial stake in. That's a job for my accountant, and let me tell you, he earns every dollar he charges me."

"That's very noble of you," I decided. "Not many people would be willing to support their friends financially."

"I can see you're curious," Jillian told me.

"Curious about what?" I wanted to know.

"How much Michael must have left me in order to

keep continually starting up businesses."

I shook my head. "No worries. I meant what I said. It is none of my business."

"Think of me as a female Richie Rich."

My eyebrows shot up. I figured she must have been loaded, but Richie Rich rich? Was she serious? Holy cow.

"Wow. You're not exaggerating? Why did you tell me that? That isn't something I necessarily need to know."

"You're you," Jillian said, by way of answer. "And it's only for your ears. I trust you. Implicitly."

I nodded and stepped out of the Gator. I offered my hand to her as she went to step down.

"Your secret is safe with me. Have you always wanted to open a bed and breakfast?"

Jillian nodded. "Believe it or not, I have. I guess I'm attracted to the old-fashioned way of caring for guests. Don't get me wrong, I don't think I have the temperament to run it myself, although I know I could if I had to."

"What made you choose Highland House?"

"It's a gorgeous house and I think it has so much potential," Jillian answered. "It has sat vacant for so long that I just want to see it fully restored and looking the way it did during its heyday."

"And when was that?" I asked.

"You've heard of the Roaring Twenties?"

I nodded. "Of course. Who hasn't?"

"Highland House has a lot of history, dating all the way back to the '20s and '30s. Did you know that it's rumored to be haunted?"

"Pssssht," I scoffed. "There's no such thing."

"I agree, yet there have been supposed sightings and disturbances for decades."

"I'd say it was just people's imaginations running away with them."

Jillian gave me an approving smile, "That's what I think, too. When my realtor called me to say that my offer had been accepted on Highland House, well, I knew it was meant to be. I have the means to restore that house to its full glory and I mean to do that. With a few modern upgrades, of course."

"Good for you. I'm sure it'll become the talk of the town once more. I rather like the idea of preventing a piece of history from fading into obscurity."

"Fading into obscurity?" Jillian repeated, giggling. "I like that. Might have to get that printed on a pamphlet."

"Ha ha."

"So, can I ask you what you think about B&Bs?"

I shrugged. "To be honest, I don't really think they're my thing."

"Can I ask you why?"

"Bathrooms, I think."

"It will have running water," Jillian assured me, with a twinkle in her eye.

"Sorry, I should have elaborated. I know it'll have running water, and plumbing. What I meant was, I'm not keen on sharing bathrooms with strangers. Now, I'm okay with sitting down at a large table and having dinner with some people I don't know, but the last thing I want to do is share a bar of soap with someone, or find a fingernail clipping on the counter, or…"

"Okay, okay, you've made your point," Jillian squeezed out, between laughs. "However, I should inform you that most of the rooms on the second floor already have bathrooms. I think there's just a few that have Jack and Jill bathrooms. It wouldn't take much to split them up. I like this. Thank you, Zachary. Is there anything else you can think of?"

"Well, if you're asking me, then I'd have to say … make Highland House pet friendly. People like traveling with their pets, and they always enjoy finding a good place that welcomes their furry companions with open arms."

"Allow pets," Jillian repeated, as she nodded. "You're turning out to be a veritable treasure trove of information. I like it. I wish I had a notebook or something to jot these ideas down."

I produced a small notebook from my back pocket and held it out to her. There was even a tiny pen clipped to the inside.

"You're dating a writer. I typically have a notebook of some fashion on me at all times. You never know when inspiration will strike."

"What would you think about retaining the haunted motif?"

Surprised, I turned to my girlfriend and gave her an appraising stare.

"What?" Jillian asked.

"Didn't they make a movie about that? *High Spirits*, with Steve Guttenberg. The movie was about a guy who tried to make others believe a castle was haunted."

"Only, it turned out it *was* haunted," Jillian added, with a coy smile.

"You've seen it! Oh, I'm so impressed. Wouldn't that be cool, though? If your Highland House was actually haunted? Man, you'd have to sign me up to be your first guest if that was true."

Jillian's phone rang. She pulled her cell out of her purse,

gave the display a quick glance, and then answered it.

"Hello, Robert. How is everything proceeding? I … what? What's that? Oh, no! Are you serious? Oh, that's terrible! What will … no. No, absolutely not. Zack and I are on our way."

"What's going on?" I asked, as soon as Jillian was off the phone.

I knew something bad had happened, because Jillian's eyes had filled with tears.

"That was Robert," Jillian sniffed, as she pulled a tissue from her purse. She hastily dabbed her eyes before taking my hand and pulling me toward the house. "He's the foreman overseeing the renovations at Highland House. Last week, one of the contractors was electrocuted."

"Jeez, that's terrible!" I agreed.

"It happened while a group of kids were taking a field trip right in front of the house."

"Oh, man," I moaned. "That can't be good."

"Thankfully, both of the teachers kept their wits about them, kept the children calm, and were able to call for an ambulance."

"The poor guy. I can't imagine what his family is going through right about now."

"Oh, he survived," Jillian said, as we hurried up the steps into my house. "Don't get me wrong, getting electrocuted is never a good thing, but at least it wasn't fatal."

"This happened last week and they're just now telling you about it?" I demanded, growing angry. "Why did they take so long to tell you? You're the owner of that building, aren't you? Aren't you entitled to be told the instant it happened?"

"I already knew about it," Jillian confessed, as she

pulled two leashes off their hooks by the door. By this time, both of the dogs had awoken from where they had been sleeping on the couch and were watching us with concerned expressions. "Sherlock? Watson? Come on. Want to go for a ride?"

The dogs executed simultaneous leaps from the couch and bounded over to us. Once the leashes were clipped on, we headed back outside. I pointed at my Jeep and then at Jillian's SUV."

"Want me to drive or would you like to?"

"You drive. Please."

"You were saying?" I said, once we had pulled away. "Something else has clearly happened. What's going on? Has someone else been hurt?"

"There's been another accident," Jillian softly told me. "This time ... this time there's been a death."

TWO

Jillian and I drove non-stop, straight to Highland House. As we pulled in front of the house and parked, alongside of Oregon Street, I couldn't help but question her choice of investments. This was the house that she had purchased? I must have driven by this thing countless times without so much as giving it a second's thought. However, Jillian must have noticed the potential in the house, because from the number of vans, trucks, and equipment outside the house, she was sinking a lot of money into its renovation.

Thankfully, the drive from my house into town was long enough to allow Jillian to calm down. She had placed a few more calls, and even texted a few people, but at least her eyes were clear. In fact, if I didn't know any better, I'd say a firm resolve had settled over her features. Was it me, or did Jillian suspect foul play?

"Highland House was built in the late 19th century," Jillian told me, as we exited my Jeep. "It's a wonderful example of a Victorian Italianate villa, which is what attracted me to it in the first place."

"Victorian Italian something-or-other?" I repeated, as I looked at her. "Tell me you didn't just make that up."

Jillian offered me a smile and shook her head. "Actually, I didn't. Victorian Italianate is a style of architecture that first became popular in England at the beginning of the 18th century. Here in the United States, it didn't catch on until 1840s, and then, only up through the 1890s, I believe. Want to know what I like most about the style?"

I nodded. "Sure."

"The corbels."

"The *what*?"

Jillian pointed up at the roof and then singled out the corner closest to us. There, just under the roofline, a carved piece of wood jutted out from the wall, looking like it was just an oversized ornate bracket. To me, it looked as though the bracket was only there to hold the weight of the roof, but why they had to make it so detailed was beyond me. A quick check of the other corner that I could see confirmed there was a similar bracket there, too.

"Are you talking about those big carved things up there in the corner?" I asked.

Jillian nodded. "Yes! I think they're spectacular. What about the windows? Do you see how the first-floor windows are so much larger than on the second floor?"

"Now that you mention it, I do."

"That means this house has a *piano nobile*. It means the first floor contains the principal reception and main bedrooms of the house."

"How do you know so much about this stuff?" I incredulously asked.

I set both dogs on the ground and, together, we stepped away from my Jeep. As we slowly walked up the steps of the house, I noticed some scaffolding along the left side of the house. How far it extended, I didn't know. A quick check on the right confirmed that the scaffolding didn't extend all the way around. An ambulance and two fire trucks were parked along the street and, thanks to the front door being wide open, I could see uniformed medics walking around inside. A familiar form materialized in front of me, and he was holding a notebook.

"Hey there, Zack. Hello, Jillian."

"No offense, Vance," I began, "but you are *not* a sight for sore eyes."

Vance Samuelson is one of my good friends here in town. He just so happens to be a detective in the Pomme Valley Police Department. We first met when he, er, arrested me for murder. Yes, it was mistake. No, I didn't do it. Thankfully, that's a story I've already told and don't need to tell again. Sure, I can laugh now, but I wasn't back then. Vance was also solely responsible for getting me involved with solving criminal cases. Well, getting the dogs involved, that is. Vance is a few years younger than me, has sandy brown hair, and is a few inches shorter as well.

Vance nodded. "No offense taken. It's mandatory, I'm afraid. Plus, in situations like these, an inspector has to come and check everything out. See if he can determine what was responsible, that sort of thing."

"I understand," Jillian said.

"It was just an accident, wasn't it?" I asked, as I looked

up at my friend. "Tell me you came over here for no reason."

"That's what I'm waiting for the inspector to tell me. He arrived about fifteen minutes ago and is presently somewhere inside the house."

"Where'd the accident happen?" I asked. "And did they... er, have they removed the, uh..."

Vance hooked a thumb toward the rear of the house.

"It happened outside, on the other side of the house. It had something to do with the scaffolding. That's all anyone has told me for now. And yes, Zack, the dead body has been removed."

Feeling tugs on the leashes, I looked down. Knowing Sherlock and Watson as well as I do, I assumed they'd want to go check out the area around back where the accident had occurred. But, did they? Nope. Sherlock wanted to go inside. In a matter of moments, both dogs morphed into their Clydesdale likenesses and tried to forcefully take me to where they wanted to go.

"Knock it off, you two. This isn't pre-meditated murder. It's only an accident."

How wrong I was. More on that in just a bit.

We looked at the overall activity of the house itself. Well, what we could see through the doorway, that is. Sherlock tugged on his leash, as though he expected to be allowed into the house to begin his own investigation. Watson, for her part, had apparently tired of waiting for us to do something, so she stretched out on the porch and was content to watch what was happening from the ground.

A short, muscular Hispanic guy in his mid-thirties appeared in the doorway. He was wearing blue overalls, a belt full of tools around his waist, an orange safety jacket, and a bright yellow hard hat. He noticed Jillian standing next to me and hurried over to her side, taking off his hat as he exited the house.

"Ms. Cooper," the man hesitantly began, "I can't even begin to imagine how to explain what happened."

Ah. This had to be Robert, the foreman. I held out a hand.

"Zack Anderson," I said, introducing myself. "You're Robert? Can you tell us what happened?"

Robert sighed heavily, ran a hand down his face, and then noticed I was holding leashes. His gaze traveled down to land on the dogs. A brief smile appeared on his face as he squatted down to give the corgis a few pats on their heads.

"I know who you are, Mr. Anderson. I've heard a lot about you, sir. And, of course, these two are Sherlock and Watson."

Upon hearing her name, Watson rose to her feet.

"Robert Sanchez. I'm the foreman here."

"Pleased to meet you, Robert. I wish it was under better circumstances."

"You and me both," Robert muttered. "I love your wine. My wife, too."

I nodded appreciatively. "What happened? Do you know?"

Robert looked back at Jillian and his face hardened.

"First off, Ms. Cooper, I want to let you know that I take everyone's safety seriously. All safety protocols have been observed. I go through and check everything, and I do mean *everything,* twice a day: first thing in the morning, and again at night, when everyone leaves."

"Was it another electrocution?" Jillian quietly asked.

Robert shook his head. "No. It was nothing like that. And even then, the electrical circuits were not overloaded. The inspector insisted it was faulty wiring on the band saw's plug, but I know for a fact that there was nothing wrong with it earlier in the day. As for today, it was the scaffolding. It collapsed."

"It collapsed?" I repeated, puzzled. "Aren't there safety precautions in place to prevent such a thing from happening?"

"Yes," Robert reported.

"By chance, was it overloaded?" Jillian asked.

Robert vehemently shook his head. "Nowhere close, ma'am. I only had one guy up there, and he was working on removing the siding from the house. You should know, those scaffolds are rated to hold 875 pounds. That's the equivalent of three guys weighing approximately 250 pounds each and 125 pounds of supplies."

"If he was removing siding," I began, "then he might have had a few tools, but probably nothing else. It couldn't possibly have been a weight issue."

Robert nodded and gave me a thumbs up, "My sentiments exactly. Thank you."

A string of men began exiting the building. Tool belts were draped over their shoulders and a various mix of power tools were seen clutched in their hands.

"Hey!" Robert called, as the men filed past us. "What are you guys doing? Where do you think you are going?"

"You can keep your pay," one man flatly stated, without bothering to turn around. "Life is too short, pal. I'll find work elsewhere."

"This was an accident," Robert called back. "Plain and simple!"

One of the men, a dark-skinned man in his fifties, stopped in front of Robert and apologetically shook his hand.

"I'm sorry, sir. I have to side with the guys. This was no accident. Scaffolding doesn't just collapse like that."

"What do you mean?" I wanted to know.

The contractor looked at me and then set his tools down. He noticed the two dogs staring up at him and gave each of them a friendly scratching behind their ears. I swear both dogs drooled a little.

"If you think about how the scaffolding is assembled," the worker began, "then you should have an idea how difficult it'd be to have it collapse, like a house of cards. The outer frames have reinforced welds to prevent breakage. There are crossbars in place to help keep it steady and secure. The planking is bolted in place so there's no chance of it moving around when you're walking. So, of all the scaffolding accidents I've ever heard about, none of it has ever collapsed straight down like that. Maybe a single weld might break, or perhaps a board snaps in half, but it's rare. This? No, this thing collapsed inward, as though all the supports gave out at the same time. It's like buying a new car and having everything go out on it at the same time. It just doesn't happen. This is something I won't ever forget for as long as I live."

"And you saw the collapse happen?" Vance skeptically asked. "How, if you don't mind me asking?"

The contractor turned to point up at the top of the house.

"I'm a roofer. I was called in to check the status of the slate roof. I was up there, inspecting several of the tiles. I knew someone was just below me, on the scaffolding, but he wasn't on my team, so I paid him no mind. I had just discovered a couple of broken tiles, so I looked over the edge to see if my partner was still on the ground, watching me. And he wasn't, by the way. That's when it happened. The scaffolding shuddered, and then collapsed straight down."

"Where was your partner?" Robert suddenly asked, frowning. "He shouldn't have left you alone like that. But, perhaps he spotted something?"

"I already asked. The fool decided to take a bathroom break, with me on the roof. Oh, I gave him hell for it and I'll be reporting him to my boss. We don't screw around with safety."

I surreptitiously glanced at Vance and noticed he was jotting a few notes into his notebook.

"What do you think happened to it to cause it to collapse the way it did?" I asked. "It sounds to me as though you have an opinion."

The roofer turned to watch the stream of workers file out of the house.

"I think the same thing they're all thinking."

"And what's that?" Jillian quietly asked, as though she knew the answer and was dreading it.

"They all think *she* is behind this, and I'm inclined to agree."

With that, the contractor walked off, leaving the four of us staring at each other with uncertain looks on our faces.

"I'm going to go talk to them," Robert announced. "I need to see if I can nip this nonsense in the bud before it gets out of control."

Jillian offered the foreman a smile, "Thank you, Robert."

I slowly raised a hand. Jillian, of course, was there to

push it back down.

"What is it, Zachary?"

"She? Which *she* is he talking about? Wait. Is he talking about the previous owner of this place? Mrs. Whatshername?"

"Dame Hilda Highland," Jillian corrected.

"Right. That's her. So, all those people, who left the house … the contractors … they all think that Dame Highland's ghost is responsible for this?"

"It certainly looks that way," Vance said, as he turned to look at the steady stream of cars that were pulling away from the house.

Concerned, I looked back at Jillian, eager to see how she was taking all of this. Jillian had a look of resolve on her face that spoke volumes. Apparently, she ain't afraid of no ghost.

Sorry. I couldn't help myself. What I meant to say was, here was a lady who wasn't about to be scared off by a silly superstition, or story, or whatever else may be at the heart of it. I, for one, was proud of her.

"I can't believe," I began, growing angry, "in this day and age that grown men—adults!—are actually afraid of ghosts. Yeah, there was a terrible accident, but it had nothing to do with some supernatural being."

Right about then, a big bald black guy exited the front door and walked across the terrace, heading directly for us. He was wearing a red short-sleeve dress shirt, blue jeans, black work boots, and sported an orange hard hat on his head. Strapped around his waist was a tool belt with a variety of gadgets and gizmos that I was unable to recognize. He was also holding a clipboard. He looked at Jillian and held out a hand.

"Ms. Cooper? I'm Jerry Springer."

Before I could stop myself, I snorted with amusement. The big guy looked at me and grinned.

"I'm sorry," I apologized. "I shouldn't have done that."

"I get it all the time," Mr. Springer explained. "If only my mother knew there'd be a famous trash talkin' white guy on TV by that name, then I think she would have reconsidered her choice. Anyway, I assume you're Ms. Jillian Cooper?" the inspector asked, as he turned to Jillian.

Jillian held up a hand, "Yes, that's me. What can I do for you, Mr. Springer?"

"I'm with the PV Building Inspection Department. I hate to do this to you, but I have to shut this site down until I can do a full and complete inspection. We need to know what caused the accident today."

Jillian's eyes filled again and she nodded.

"I understand, Mr. Springer. I would also like to know what happened. So please, take all the time you need."

Jerry took a step back and stared at Jillian with astonishment written all over his face.

"Really? You're not going to cop an attitude with me, or insinuate that I need to be done by a certain time? I'll be damned."

"I take it you hear that a lot," I murmured.

Jerry nodded. "Like, on a daily basis. All right, folks. If you could get everyone to clear out, then I'll get to work."

"Out of curiosity, how long do these inspections typically take?" I asked.

Jerry shrugged. "It obviously depends on the property. On average, I usually get each inspection done in an hour or two. Since I'm investigating an accident on a work site, I'll need to be more thorough. I have to check everything, so I'd give me a day or two to get it done."

Jillian nodded. "Of course."

Robert reappeared then, and the look on his face wasn't promising.

"No luck?" I guessed.

"The men are all refusing to step back inside the house," the foreman angrily confirmed. "I told them that this was just a freak accident, but they won't listen. You'd think I was working with a group of *pendejos*."

While I wasn't exactly sure what Robert had said, I could tell from the way Vance started grinning that, whatever a pendejo was, it was some sort of insult. I looked over at Jillian, but she wasn't smiling. Clearly, my detective friend spoke a little Spanish. I'd have to ask him about that later.

"Did you tell them that they weren't expected to go back in right now, but in a couple of days, when the safety inspector has finished his job?" Jillian asked.

Robert nodded. "I did, yeah. Didn't do any good, though."

"Okay, let me ask you something, Robert," I said, as I stepped forward. "Did you see anything in there that appeared, I don't know, out of the ordinary?"

Robert met my eyes and held them for a few moments.

"Are you asking if I saw her? No, amigo, I did not. I didn't hear anything and I didn't see anything. If I did, you'd be the first to know. Did the inspector say how long it'll be before we can get back to work?"

"A few days, probably," Jillian answered.

"That'll give me time to get some people back in here. Gracias, señora. I'll be in touch."

"Thank you, Robert."

"*¡Aye, caramba!*" Robert muttered, as he walked down

the steps. *"Mi equipo no es más que pendejos grandes."*

We all watched as the foreman unlocked a newer model Chevy Silverado crew cab truck and drive away.

"Anyone know what he said as he left?" I asked.

Vance chuckled, "Essentially, he was complaining that he works with a bunch of stupid idiots."

Jillian turned to Vance, "I did not realize you spoke Spanish, Vance."

The detective shrugged. "I learned it in high school. I don't really get a chance to use it too much."

I looked at Jillian and hooked a thumb back at the house.

"Okay, what do we know about this Dame Highland person? For the sake of argument, let's just assume that she's here, as a ghost. Now I realize that all the information I know about ghosts are based on movies, but aren't ghosts here because they have refused to move on? Do we know what happened to her?"

Jillian somberly nodded. "I know a little. Dame Highland was murdered in this house a long time ago. Since then, there have been dozens of reported sightings, in various parts of the house."

"Ghost sightings?" Vance hesitantly asked.

Jillian nodded. "That's right. Highland House, I'm sorry to say, is rumored to be the most haunted house in all the state."

"That explains the contractors' reluctance to go back to work," I sourly observed.

My girlfriend had just purchased a haunted house. That's just peachy.

THREE

Two uneventful days passed. I stopped by Cookbook Nook on what had come to be known as my daily foraging session. For soda. I know, I know. I could have saved a lot of money had I just bought cans of soda and kept them at home, in the fridge. However, heading out practically every day to Wired Coffee & Café, just to buy a soda, gave me a perfect excuse to stop by a certain specialty book store and see my girlfriend.

Honestly, I never thought I'd be feeling like a love-struck teenager, not after losing my childhood sweetheart in a horrible car accident a few years ago. Neither could Jillian, for that matter. She had lost her husband to cancer, and neither one of us expected to fall this hard for another person. However, the two of us hit it off from the start and the rest, as they say, is history.

Holding my mega 96-ounce mug of soda in one hand, and Jillian's iced blended chai soybean drink in the other, *and* managing to keep Sherlock and Watson from yanking either drink out of my hand, we made it inside. Hurrying over to the counter so I could set both drinks down before they spilled, I cast a stern look at the dogs. Both corgis were staring up at me, as if to say, *not bad for a human. We'll get you next time.*

"That was close, guys. Too close. Do you know how much of a mess that would've made had I dropped my soda?"

"Five gallons of soda would have definitely made a mess," a female voice quipped from behind me.

Turning, I saw a young redheaded teenage girl eyeing me with a smile on her face. However, the smile wasn't for me, but for the dogs. The girl wearing the purple apron dropped to one knee and gave both dogs a hearty scratching.

"We thought for certain you were going to drop them this time," the girl told me.

"Thanks for the support, kiddo," I joked. Then, a thought occurred. "Hey, you haven't placed any wagers on me, have you?"

"About when you'll drop something coming in the door?" the girl mischievously asked. She winked. "I have next Friday, around noon. Katherine has the following Monday."

I rolled my eyes. "Thanks a lot. Could you point out where I might find Jillian? Is she in her office?"

The girl, Sydney, pointed upstairs, "No, she's in the café. Umm, I'll watch your dogs if you want to go up there."

Familiar with Jillian's staff watching the corgis whenever I showed up, and since health regulations forbid any type of animals from entering a commercial kitchen, I wordlessly passed the leashes over. The girl cooed at the dogs before turning on her heel and walking further into the heart of the store. Neither dog, I should point out, bothered to look back at me. What that was supposed to mean, I'd rather not know.

"Zachary!" Jillian exclaimed, as she looked up from a table covered with paperwork. "What a pleasant surprise!"

I thought back to the girls downstairs and shrugged. "Apparently not."

"Oh, don't let those two intimidate you," Jillian teased. "They know you're here because of me, and they're just trying to get your goat."

"Hey, I'm not afraid of a couple of teeny-boppers," I clarified.

"They told you about the betting pool, didn't they?"

I sighed. "Apparently, I'm not as mysterious as I used to be."

"Only if you don't spill the drinks this coming Friday or the following Monday. Wait. Was it today? Did you spill the drinks today? Hmm, they still look pretty full."

"That's because I *didn't* spill them. You sound as though you have today's date covered."

Jillian smiled sheepishly at me.

"Oh, lord. You do, don't you?"

"I may have purchased a few of the open days," Jillian confessed. Her eyes sparkled with amusement. "So, Zachary, you do realize tonight is movie night, don't you?"

I nodded. "I do. It's my turn to pick the movie, isn't it?"

"Nice try," Jillian laughed. "After subjecting me to over

two hours of killer cyborgs trying to mutilate one another, I think it's safe to say I get to choose next."

My head tilted as I stared at her.

"Nuh-uh. The last movie we watched was a chick flick. Something about a bunch of ladies who liked to get drunk every single night and try to relive their youth. It's my turn, woman."

Jillian stared at me for a few moments.

"It was cyborgs," she insisted.

"Drunk chicks," I returned.

After a few moments of staring at one another, we both held up a clenched hand. I'm not sure what the point of this was supposed to be. I never win these things.

"One … two … three. Hah! Scissors cuts paper! I win, Zachary!"

Why do I even bother trying? To date, we've had about a dozen of these rock-paper-scissor sessions, and do you want to know how many of them I've won? Not a single one. After this many attempts, the odds should be in my favor, but clearly Jillian is employing some trick where she manages to figure out what I'm gonna do before I can even do it.

Oh, well. Sappy romance it is. I was about ready to ask Jillian what was on the docket for tonight when I heard a sharp, exasperated bark. Curious, I leaned back in my chair and looked down the stairs. It wasn't a direct line to the cashier station, where I knew Sydney had the dogs, but it was close. I was just in time to see a streak of tri-colored fur zip by. Thankfully, Sherlock wasn't heading for the door, and oddly enough, he wasn't headed up here, either, but further into the store.

"Was that Sherlock?" Jillian asked. "Is he okay?"

"I think so. I just saw him go running by, with Sydney in hot pursuit. I know that bark. He wants something, and he's frustrated his intentions aren't clear enough for us stupid bipeds to figure out."

Jillian giggled, "Stupid bipeds, huh?"

"Got a better way to describe it?" I grinned. "I'll see what he's up to. I'll be right back."

"Hurry back. I can't wait to tell you about the movie I've selected for tonight. And no, it's not a romance movie. It's a classic French film."

"But, I don't speak French!"

"Oh, don't worry. There are subtitles."

"Swell. You're trying to get even with me. I'm not sure why."

Jillian laughed. "That cyborg lady had knives for hands! And she was trying to hurt that poor little girl! I'll probably have nightmares for months."

"Oh, please," I scoffed. "That 'little girl' kicked the ever- lovin' snot out of the cyborg. She wasn't hurt in the slightest. Besides, she was a cyborg, too!"

"However you explain it, you'll have to admit it was a strange movie. The girl's eyes bothered me. Too big."

"Done on purpose," I laughed. "We've been through this. It's to honor the story's Japanese manga background."

"You'll love this one," Jillian assured me. "I promise."

"I'll hold you to it," I called back to her, as I headed down the stairs. "Sherlock? Watson? Where are you two?"

"They keep slipping away from me!" Sydney told me, in an exasperated tone. I watched her hurry by for a second time. "I'm not sure what's going on. I never knew Sherlock was so good at sneaking away. And I swear, he's showing Watson how to do it."

"I wouldn't put it past him," I laughed. "Okay, you go that way, and I'll go this way. He's gotta be here somewhere."

The high school teen moved off, walking parallel to the store front. I headed through tall cases of books, intent on making as little noise as possible. *Cookbook Nook* had linoleum floors. I should easily be able to hear the clicking of doggie toe nails, provided they were still moving around. The problem was, it was relatively quiet in the store, and I didn't hear any movement whatsoever.

"Come on guys," I quietly murmured. "Give me a sign. Jingle a collar, let out a woof, anything!"

"I found them, Mr. Anderson," Sydney called, from the other side of the store. "They're over by the Specialty Cakes section."

"Specialty cakes?" I softly repeated.

Were there really that many books about specialty cakes that Jillian had to create its own section? I arrived a few moments later to find Sydney holding both leashes and trying to give Sherlock a stern scolding. Both corgis were sitting on their rumps and were paying the teenage girl absolutely no mind. They seemed to be looking at the picture on the wall next to the display. All I could see was a couple of children, walking hand-in-hand, down a path through a thick forest. A small cottage was nearby, and there was a wisp of smoke wafting up from the chimney. Whatever. I walked up in time to see Sherlock look my way and, if possible, give me a sheepish grin.

"What are you doing, pal?" I asked, as I squatted down next to the dogs. I draped an arm around each of them and gave them a good scratching. "Since when is it like you two to go running off like that?"

I started walking, intent on leading them away from the

display of custom cake decorating books when I felt both leashes become taut. I gave them a gentle tug, to indicate we were headed in a different direction, when I heard Sherlock snort and shake his collar. A few moments later, both were walking next to me.

"You want me to take up cake decorating?" I asked the dogs, as we headed toward the back of the building. This was after I had noticed Jillian had finally come down the stairs and was headed for her office. "I don't think I'd be any good at it."

Jillian appeared a few moments later. Her purse had been slung over her shoulder and she had her keys in her hand.

"Ready for lunch?"

Both dogs perked up at this.

"She's asking me, not you two," I told the dogs.

It didn't matter. The dogs knew we were about to go for a ride and were thrilled they were included. Oh, I should mention something before you start wondering about PV's restaurants. Many of the businesses situated along Main Street had open air terraces. Most, if not all, of the restaurants allowed the dogs to come onto the terrace and sit with their owners while they had a bite to eat. The stickler was, the dogs—obviously—were not allowed into the actual restaurant. So, with that being said, the four of us drove to one of my favorite places to eat, Casa de Joe's. It might not sound like an authentic Mexican restaurant, but let me assure you, it was, hands down, the best place to cure a burrito craving within a hundred mile radius. Mexican food has to be one of my favorite types of food, and I can say that I've frequented a lot of restaurants, especially in the Phoenix, Arizona area. However, not even the places in Arizona, serving *authentic* Mexican food, could hold their own against *Casa de Joe's*. Trust me, it was that good.

"I'm beginning to think it was a mistake to purchase Highland House," Jillian sullenly began, after the waitress had taken our orders and placed a bowl of chips in front of us. "I don't know, Zachary. I'm starting to think the place is cursed after all."

I was silent as I munched on a few chips. I knew this was currently a delicate situation for her, especially since someone had died in that house, while working for *her*. You'd have to understand my girlfriend. She had to be the most caring, sweetest person I have ever encountered. This was someone who would actually catch and release bugs outside before she'd ever kill one. So, in this situation, I knew that the accident, even though it *was* an accident, weighed heavily on her mind. Now, it would seem, she was looking for my take on the situation and I was more than happy to give it.

"Look, it was just an accident," I began. "These sorts of things can and do happen. I'm not saying it's a good thing, not at all. But, don't let it dissuade you from doing what you want. Highland House is going to look fan-freakin'-tastic after it's been restored. It'll be the talk of the town, trust me."

Jillian laid a hand over mine.

"Thank you. I needed to hear that. That house has already seen someone else die in it. I just don't want to see anyone else get hurt."

"You're referring to what's-her-face, Dame Highland, right? You said she was killed in her own house? Do you know how it happened?"

Jillian shrugged. "Not really. I only know that the

previous owner lived in that house up until her death and it has sat vacant ever since."

"And when was that?" I wanted to know.

"Umm, I'm not sure. I think it was in the '50s."

"1947," a young female voice corrected.

We both looked up. Our waitress, a cute brunette with a strong girl-next-door vibe about her, who I guessed was in her early twenties, was standing before us. This particular girl had waited on the two of us numerous times in the past and was known to be a very efficient worker. Considering how we'd already placed our orders, and since both of us did not need a refill on our drinks, this girl must have overheard our conversation and stopped to offer an opinion.

"You're guessing?" I asked.

The girl—Sammi by her name tag—shook her head.

"You're talking about what happened at Highland House, right? About when Dame Highland was murdered? It was 1947. I did a research paper on it last year, for school. Did I hear that right? Did you really buy that house?"

Jillian nodded. "I did. Let's keep that between ourselves, okay?"

The girl nodded enthusiastically.

"You can count on me, Ms. Cooper."

Our waitress was given a school project *and* decided to focus her paper on Jillian's newest acquisition? You couldn't ask for better timing than that. Hopefully she'd be able to shed some light on what happened.

"Do you have a few minutes?" I eagerly asked. "What can you tell us about it?"

"Well, like I said earlier, Dame Highland was killed in 1947," Sammi began. "There were two suspects, both of whom were vagrants living in the area. The only thing that was listed in the police report was that they figured these two bums learned of Dame Highland's extensive jewelry collection, and wanted it for themselves. Whether or not they got it, no one knows, but the police figured they didn't."

"Didn't what?" I asked. "Get the jewels? How would they know?"

"Nothing ever turned up," Sammi informed me. She noticed the dwindling number of chips in our bowl and pointed at it. "Would you like some more chips?"

"I believe we would. Wait. Is there something I don't know? Have you guys started charging for extra chips?"

Sammi grinned. "Nope. Unless you need a refill on your salsa, that is. Be right back."

I looked at the half-full bowl of salsa and grunted.

"I don't know if she's serious or not."

Sammi was back in less than thirty seconds.

"Here you go. Now, where were we?"

"You mentioned the jewelry never turned up," I reminded our waitress. "So, the logical assumption is that they were unable to get the location out of her."

Sammi nodded. "Right. That's what I think happened, too."

"So, they killed her because she wouldn't tell those two men where her jewelry was," Jillian repeated. She frowned a few moments later. "I hope they were caught."

Sammi shook her head. "They weren't, I'm sorry to say. They got away, only based on what I read in the police report, they didn't make it too far. They were discovered a week later in Medford."

"Discovered, and not apprehended?" I asked, confused.

Sammi nodded. "Yes. They were both dead. According to the Medford police report that I managed to get a copy of, it was decided that each man turned on the other."

"Doesn't that suggest that they found at least a few pieces of jewelry?" I asked. "If they turned on each other, then wouldn't that mean each person wanted what the other had?"

"Not necessarily," Jillian argued. "Maybe they were scared. Maybe one of them suggested they turned themselves in, and the other didn't want to?"

I had to concede the point.

"Okay, sure. That's one way to look at it. Either way, there was a lady who had way too much jewelry."

Noticing the table had fallen deathly quiet, I turned to see Jillian staring at me with an unreadable expression. Then I looked at Sammi and saw the same expression on her young face. I was suddenly surprised at how hard my seat had become and fidgeted restlessly.

"A girl can never have too much jewelry," Jillian scolded. She turned to Sammi and winked at her. "Don't ever let a boy tell you otherwise."

Sammi grinned. "You got it, Ms. Cooper."

When the girl didn't offer any additional details, I gave her an expectant look and calmly waited for her to continue. When she didn't, I cleared my throat and fidgeted in my chair.

"Is there anything else you can tell us?"

Sammi produced a menu and slid it over to me.

"What's this for? We've already placed our orders."

"I thought that, perhaps, you'd like to order an appetizer or two while you were waiting."

I pushed the menu back toward the girl.

"No, thanks. Now, about Dame Highland. What more can you tell us?"

The menu was pushed back over to me.

"Really? Are you sure you wouldn't like to try an appetizer? The mini carne asada tostadas are *sooo* good!"

I looked at the girl and felt a smile spread across my face. It had just dawned on me what she was doing. I order something *else* from the menu, and she divulges another juicy bit of info from her research paper.

Clever snot.

Wordlessly, I slid the menu closer and flipped it open. I checked the ingredients on the suggested tostadas and nodded approvingly. They *did* sound good. I glanced at Jillian and saw that she was pretending to look at her phone.

"All right. Let's try the mini tostadas. Now, you were saying?"

"Would you like a side of guacamole with that?"

"Is it extra?" I asked, already knowing the answer.

The girl nodded enthusiastically, "Yes, but it's only a dollar."

"Are you getting a kickback from this place?" I good-naturedly asked.

Sammi gave me another smile and shrugged her shoulders.

"Perhaps."

"And how did you swing that?" I asked, impressed. "You must be one helluva negotiator."

"Well, my aunt and uncle own the place."

"Ah."

"Now, what else would you like to know?"

"Whatever you can tell us would be great," I replied.

Sammi nodded. "Okay. As you may have guessed, Ms.

Hilda Highland was a very wealthy woman. She was the sole beneficiary of her late father's fortune."

"Who was her father?" Jillian asked. "What did he do?"

"She was the only daughter of Harrison Highland. I know he was a colonel, or some type of officer, in some war, but I forget which one."

And this girl wrote a research paper?

"Did Dame Highland ever marry?"

Sammi shook her head. "No. At least, not according to the records I checked. Birth, death, marriage, census. There was never any mention of kids. I do remember reading she had quite a few suitors, but she wasn't interested."

"Did she have any other surviving family members?" I asked.

The menu was produced again, and once more, slid over to me.

"Can I interest you in a dessert tonight?"

"Man, we haven't even received our entrees yet," I protested.

"I'm just making sure you leave room for dessert," Sammi said, with mock innocence. "Our caramel empanadas are out of this world."

I heard a giggle. A quick check of my girlfriend confirmed that she had become, once more, engrossed with her phone.

"Sure, why not? You're gonna have to roll my fat butt out of here."

It was Sammi's turn to giggle.

"Oh, you don't need to worry about that, Mr. Anderson."

So, she knew my name after all?

"We have a general purpose dolly in the back, and it'll

hold a thousand pounds. You should be okay."

The smile on my face disappeared in the blink of an eye, only to reappear on Jillian's face a split second later.

"No comments from the peanut gallery," I told her, as I waggled a finger at her. "Now, Ms. Smarty-Pants, you were saying? Are there any other family members?"

"Dame Highland had an aunt," Sammi dutifully reported. "She married and had several kids. The last I heard, a granddaughter of hers was still alive, and living in Bremerton."

"Where's that?" I wanted to know.

"Washington State," Jillian answered. "Thank you, Sammi. You've been most helpful."

The girl nodded and immediately headed to a nearby table, where the hostess had just seated a large family.

"Washington State," I repeated. "At least she didn't say they were living in Rhode Island. What are the chances that this granddaughter might shed some more light on Dame Highland? We might be able to find a phone number for her."

"She might have a few memories," Jillian decided. "It all depends on how old she is."

Right then, Jillian's cell phone started ringing.

"I need to remember to turn this thing off whenever we go inside a restaurant," Jillian told me, as she dug through her purse to retrieve her phone. "I don't want to be one of *those* people, namely someone who disrupts another person's dinner. Hello? Yes, this is Jillian Cooper. Who is... oh! Mr. Springer! How are you today, sir?"

Jillian muted the phone call and leaned toward me.

"It's the safety inspector."

I nodded. "I remember. He had a name you wouldn't

easily forget."

Jillian smiled at me and unmuted her phone. "Wait, what was that? Could you say that again, please?"

She fell silent as Mr. Springer evidently explained what he had found.

"On all of them? Or only on some? Just the corner pieces. I see. What do you...? No, I had no idea. All that is handled by my foreman, who ... yes, of course. I can wait."

Jillian muted the phone again and turned to me. She had a look on her face I will never forget: anger.

"What's going on?" I whispered, as I placed my hand over hers.

"The safety inspector has finished his inspection. You'll never guess what he found."

"Something about corner pieces?"

Jillian nodded. "Yes. The scaffolding that collapsed? Apparently, this particular type of scaffolding had what he called gravity locking pins, to keep it from falling apart."

I slowly nodded. "Okay. I know what you're referring to. What about them? Have they been tampered with?"

Jillian shook her head. "Worse. The pins have been removed. Zachary, someone has stolen the pins holding the scaffolding together. It was only a matter of time before the whole thing collapsed!"

"But, that's premeditated," I stammered. "That means..."

Jillian suddenly sat up straight and unmuted the phone call.

"Yes, I'm still here, Mr. Springer. No, I'm grateful you told me. I'll be sure to pass that along to my foreman. I know he'll want to know. Oh? Is it? Well, that *is* good news.

I'll call him right away. Thanks again for all of your help, Mr. Springer. Thank you. You have a good day, too."

"What's the good news?" I asked, hopeful that it'd put a smile on Jillian's face.

"The house has been cleared. Work can resume on it. Would you mind if I made another phone call? I have to let Robert know."

"Please, do what you need to do. I'm not going anywhere."

"Thank you, Zachary. It'll be just a moment. I know I've got his number in here from … ah. There it is. Hello, Robert? This is Jillian Cooper. I'm fine, thank you for asking. I wanted to know if you have spoken with the safety inspector, Mr. Jerry Springer. Yes, he called me and explained to me what he found. What's that? Yes, we know what happened. I'm sorry to say this, and something tells me you won't like hearing this, but it looks like quite a few of the scaffolding's gravity locking pins had been removed. I'm sorry, you heard that right. I … no, we … Robert? Please calm down. I know this isn't your fault. I…"

Jillian muted her phone for a third time and looked helplessly at me. Even from where I was sitting, I could hear Robert cursing and shouting, in both Spanish and English. I pointed a finger at the phone and frowned.

"Tell me he's not yelling at you."

"He's not," Jillian confirmed. "He told me he knows full well those pins were in place that morning. He did a full check of all equipment, too, before the rest of his team arrived. He … Robert? Yes, I'm still here. You … hmm? Oh. I'm sorry to hear that. How long do you need? Very well. Let's give it a few days, just to let things blow over. We'll reconvene on Monday. How does that sound?

It does? Perfect. I'll see you then."

"I'm glad he wasn't yelling at you," I said, as Jillian slipped her phone back into her purse. "I can only assume he thought you were accusing him of tampering with those pins?"

"Actually, he now thinks it's a member of his crew. He was just telling me that most of them still refuse to return to work. He sounded stressed, like he was trying to find replacements for his team."

"That's why you suggested Monday," I guessed. "That'll give him some time to get some more guys together."

"Exactly. Plus, it's also given me an idea. What would you say to a little get together?"

"With the gang?" I asked.

The gang was the circle of our immediate friends, which included Harry and his wife, Julie; Vance and his wife, Tori; and lately, we've also been including Hannah and her son, Colin. For the record, a get together this Friday might just be what the doctor ordered. For Jillian, that is. I'd really like to get her mind off this blasted house.

"Yes, we'd include everyone," Jillian confirmed.

"I can get on board with that. Do you have something in mind?"

"We're going to have a little party," Jillian explained. "At Highland House."

Oh, snap. This wasn't the distraction I figured it to be. What, then, does she have up her sleeve?

"What's on your mind? Do you … wait. You want to check out the house, don't you? Are we looking for anything in particular?"

Jillian solemnly nodded. "Yes. We'll be looking for ghosts."

FOUR

Seriously, if a spook jumps out at me, then I'm personally running straight through you, Julie, and anyone else who's stupid enough to get in my way."

The speaker, my best friend from high school, was Harrison Watt. All his friends called him Harry. He also happened to be the town veterinarian, which still blows my mind. You see, back in school, Harry was the biggest goof-off on the face of the planet. He'd been suspended from school so many times that I honestly didn't see how he managed to graduate. But, as it turns out, all he needed to turn his life around was a close brush with death—in Harry's case, a nasty car accident—and before you know it, he had a new appreciation for life.

Harry's wife, Julie, stood beside her husband and slowly

looked around the small foyer. Visible straight ahead was a curved dual set of stairs leading up to the second floor. After a few moments Jillian, pushed by Harry, walked into the main reception area.

"I call this Staircase Hall," Jillian said, as they spread out behind her. "The living room is to the left, through there. The dining room is north of it. Then, through that door behind you on the left, there's a small room for which its intended purpose is lost on me."

Julie poked her head into the room for a quick check.

"Maybe a sitting room?"

Jillian nodded. "I like it. Now, through that other doorway, on the right, is a den. Or a study, I'm not sure. Will Hannah and Colin be able to join us tonight?"

Julie shook her head. "I'm afraid not. She has another meeting with her attorney. She's fairly certain that her divorce is going to be finalized soon."

"I sure hope so," I added. "The sooner she's officially done with that loser, the better."

"Hear, hear," Tori echoed.

I pointed at the open doorway on the right, adjacent to the den.

"What's through there?"

"I really don't know," Jillian admitted. "Perhaps it was a rec room of some sort? It's certainly large enough. There's a huge kitchen on the other side of the stairs and there's plenty of storage everywhere."

"The bedrooms are all on the first floor?" Tori asked.

"Yes. There are six rooms, including the master bedroom, which I think can be split in half. That'd give us seven rooms total."

"The interior isn't too bad," Julie decided. "I like the tiling on the floor. Do you see this? It's some type of mosaic. I hope you plan on keeping this here, Jillian."

"I certainly do," Jillian confirmed. She ushered everyone into the living room. "Well, what do you guys think?"

"Ummm," Harry slowly began, as his eyes took in the dust, decay, and overall shabbiness of Highland House's living room. "You really bought this?"

"You can't look at it the way it is now," I told my friend. "You have to be able to either picture what it looked like, back in the 1920s and '30s, or else imagine what it'll look like once Jillian is done with the place. I think it's gonna look fantastic. I love the décor in here."

"You do?" Jillian excitedly asked. "What parts?"

I started pointing at various objects. "That, for starters. What is it, some type of coffee table? Look at all the carvings on it. You don't see that every day, do you?"

"There isn't much to see in here," Vance added, as he and Tori stepped further into the living room and looked around.

"The original furniture has been moved," Jillian explained. "I didn't want to risk any of the original décor becoming damaged once the renovations began."

"Why didn't you take this, then?" I asked, as I looked back at the small table.

Jillian shrugged. "Robert gave me a list of things that need to happen in this house. The order in which they're getting fixed is by the total number of code violations the room presently has. If memory serves, there was less than ten in this room, so it's about halfway down the list."

"Then why cover the furniture in here?" Vance wanted to know. "I can only imagine you'll be replacing everything, right?"

Jillian shook her head. "I'm going to have the furniture

refinished, reupholstered, and so on."

"You're keeping it as original as possible," I guessed.

Jillian smiled at me, "Precisely."

"I've always loved antiques," Tori said, as she gazed wistfully at some of the tarps covering various objects. "Would you mind if I take a look?"

Jillian held out a welcoming hand, "Please. Be my guest. Harry? Do you want to come all the way inside? Nothing will bite you, I promise."

As one, both of my dogs craned their heads to look up at Jillian. What happened next couldn't have been timed any better, even if I had tried. After staring at Jillian for a few moments, both corgis then turned to look back at Harry, who was standing just inside the open door, leading back to the foyer. Then, they both did that adorable head tilt thing dogs do if they find something puzzling. The entire room burst into laughter. Harry, unsurprisingly, was the only one who didn't find it funny.

"This house has a history, man," PV's resident veterinarian insisted. "Do you really think all those people just made up those stories for the heck of it? Think about it. There's … I don't know. There's something…"

"…afoot at the Circle K," both Vance and I interrupted, using deadpan voices at the exact same time.

We gave each other an appraising look before we bumped fists together.

"I don't get it," Tori complained. "What just happened here? Why did those two say the same nonsensical thing at the same time?"

Jillian was shaking her head.

"Boys."

"It's a line from *Bill & Ted's Excellent Adventure*," Harry explained. "Righteous movie, man. And, while I'm at it, you both can kiss my ass."

Vance and I developed a case of the chuckles.

An hour later, we were all sitting in the living room, polishing off the three large pizzas Jillian had ordered. A new pizza place had moved into town, Sarah's Pizza Parlor, and we had decided to give them a try. For the record, I'm glad we did. We ended up ordering pepperoni and sausage, a thin crust Hawaiian pizza, and finally, Jillian was delighted to learn this new pizza joint would make her favorite pizza: salami and ham, with white sauce.

The food was outstanding. Fantastic crust, fresh toppings, garlic knots worth arm wrestling over (which we did—me vs. Vance. I won!), and they were punctual. You really couldn't beat that in a pizza delivery restaurant.

"I think I found my new favorite pizza place," Vance said, as he tossed his and Tori's paper plates into the trash can. "That was really good. The last couple of pizzas I've had were almost dripping with grease."

"What do you expect when you order it with triple pepperoni?" Tori dryly asked.

Vance shrugged.

"So," Julie began, as she looked over at her friend, "we're all here, Jillian. This is your show. How do you want us to proceed?"

"How are we going to proceed with *what*?" Harry asked.

Jillian looked at Harry and smiled.

"Oh, come on, man," Harry moaned. "What have you dragged us into?"

"I'm a firm believer that there's no such thing as ghosts," Jillian began.

Heads were nodding.

"I'm sure all of you have heard what's happened here in the last couple of weeks?"

Everyone nodded. Everyone but Harry, that is.

"Wait, what? What happened in the last couple of weeks?" Harry wanted to know.

"Oh, come on," Julie teased her husband. "You can't possibly tell me you don't know. I, for one, have talked with you about it. Are you saying you've been ignoring me?"

"Umm…"

"Two weeks ago," Jillian hurriedly began, before Julie could respond, "one of the contractors I hired was electrocuted in here during the demo phase. While cutting through a wall that needed to come down, and after being told all power had been shut off, a contractor wielding a reciprocating saw was electrocuted when he hit a live power line."

"A power line that should've been shut off," Tori said, horrified. "Was he … did he…"

"He ended up being okay," Jillian assured the group. "He was held in the hospital for a day or two just to be sure. In the meantime, everyone chalked it up as being exactly like it appeared: an accident. Then … then earlier this week, there was another accident, only this time…"

"…this time," I said, picking up the story after Jillian trailed off, "there was a fatality."

"What happened?" Harry wanted to know.

"Do you see the scaffolding outside?" I said, as I pointed at a window where we could see the shadows of the bars. "It collapsed at the back of the house while there was someone on it."

The room fell silent. Sherlock whined, as if to say he was uncomfortable being in the room with so many somber people. I patted the sofa next to me and waited for the dogs to join me.

"How could scaffolding just collapse?" Harry wanted to know. "Aren't there precautions you can take which would prevent just that?"

Jillian nodded. "Yes, there are. The safety inspector conducted a thorough inspection here just after the accident happened. He determined the gravity locking pins had been removed."

"All of them?" Vance demanded, shocked.

"Not all," Jillian quietly answered. "Unfortunately, just the pins that were holding the corners together. The scaffolding, quite literally, collapsed like a house of cards."

"Why don't I know anything about this?" Vance asked, as he stared hard at Jillian. "Wouldn't this be classified as a homicide now?"

Jillian shrugged. "We don't know if the contractors forgot to insert the pins once the scaffolding had been assembled…"

"Which is malarkey," I grumbled.

"…or if the pins were deliberately removed."

"Voluntary or involuntary manslaughter," Vance said. "However you look at it, this will reflect badly on the construction company."

Jillian cleared her throat.

"I should probably tell you something. Robert, who is my foreman, by the way, insists that those pins were there at the start of the day."

"Voluntary manslaughter it is," Vance decided.

"Are we looking for those pins, is that it?" Tori asked.

"Partially," Jillian admitted. "Right now, I'm ashamed to admit that I haven't really explored this house yet. I only have been given a very brief tour with my realtor."

Both dogs whined this time. Sherlock reared up to place his front legs on the couch next to me. Questioningly, I looked over at Jillian, who nodded, giving the dogs permission to jump up on the furniture.

"It's okay, boy. We just don't want any more of those accidents. That's why we're here. More specifically, that's why you two are here. If there's anything suspicious going on in this house, then I'm counting on you two to find it."

"That's what you want us to do?" Harry asked, incredulously. "You want us to search this place?"

Jillian nodded. "That's *exactly* what I need. If I can prove to my closest friends that there aren't any supernatural anomalies in this house, then I should be able to prove that normal, regular human beings did this. I want to put this supernatural nonsense to bed once and for all."

"How do you want us to do this?" Julie asked.

"I was thinking that, perhaps, you and Harry could take…"

A loud thump sounded from nearby. It silenced the six of us instantly. I glanced down at the dogs. Both sets of ears were perked up as they curiously looked around the room, as if they were expecting to find another person present. Unfortunately, that was the *last* thing I wanted to find.

"Oh, holy hell," Harry muttered. "*I knew it!*"

Then we all heard it: a low moaning. Sherlock immediately fired off a warning woof. The tri-colored corgi then jumped down to the floor and trotted toward the foyer. After a few moments, he was back, only he was carrying something in his mouth.

"What's that?" Jillian nervously asked. "Sherlock, what

are you holding?"

"It looks like a phone," Tori observed. "In fact, it looks like..." She trailed off as she turned to stare incredulously at her husband.

"Umm, I can explain."

All heads turned to Vance, who now bore a sheepish, shit-eating grin on his face.

"It was done in good fun, that's all. Come on, Tor! It was just a harmless prank! I was just trying to lighten the situation."

"Someone died in here," Tori quietly began. "Someone lost their life, Vance. You, of all people, should know that."

"Someone's *about* to lose his," Harry quipped.

As for me? I was curious. How did Vance get his phone to play that noise from across the room? And at the right time?

As if in answer to my question, Vance held up what had to be his newest toy: a smart watch. It was obviously linked to his phone.

Tori scowled, "I never should have got you that watch for your birthday."

"In my defense, I do use it every single day," Vance said, in as soothing of a tone as I had ever heard come from him. "Granted, the timing was terrible, I see that now. But ... I'll just shut up now."

"Wise choice, mister," Tori said. Her tone had gone icy and it had become painfully obvious that Vance had some damage control to do before he was fully out of the dog house.

"As I was saying," Jillian said, as she fought to keep a straight face, "I think we should split up into teams. There's six of us, so that'll give us three teams, one for each floor.

Harry? Julie? You two take the second story. Tori? Vance?
You two take the basement. Zachary and I will take the
ground floor here."

"What do you want us to look for?" Tori asked. The
tall redhead was still shooting daggers at her husband.

"Anything out of the ordinary," Jillian reported. "A
bag full of scaffolding pins, or evidence of squatters, or
evidence of animals that might have snuck in the house,
or…"

"…evidence of ectoplasm," I interjected, drawing a
smile from Vance.

"That's not even funny, man," Harry complained.

"Just keep telling yourself that there's no such thing as
ghosts," I suggested.

As if we were a football team, and had just broken a
huddle, everyone moved off to their respective floors.

"Harry is the one we should pull a prank on," I softly
murmured.

Jillian turned to give me an unsettling look.

"Are you telling me that you'd like to end up like Vance?
Did you see how Tori was looking at him?"

I passed Watson's leash to Jillian and shook my head.

"I saw that look. And no, I would never want to be on
the receiving end, that's for sure. Now, where would you
like to start?"

Jillian pointed back toward the foyer.

"Let's start at the beginning. Watson? Would you care
to lead the way?"

The small red and white corgi got to her feet, gave
herself a vigorous shaking, and then—after glancing at
Sherlock —trotted toward the front door. We inspected
the front entrance, making certain to check for evidence

of lock tampering. Ever since PV had been visited by a professional burglar armed with what was referred to as 'bump keys', which allowed an unauthorized person to gain entry to just about any residential house, I've paid particular attention to locks. This one, thank goodness, didn't look as though it had been tampered with. Sure, it was old, and rusty, but it looked sturdy. I'm sure with a bit of spit and polish, it'd clean up nicely.

"Has it been picked?" Jillian asked, after a few minutes of silence had passed.

I straightened.

"Nope. At least, it doesn't look like it."

"Good. Okay, we've seen the living room. Let's go check on the dining room."

"Where's that again?" I asked, as we headed back into the living room. I hesitated only long enough to snag another piece of pizza. Jillian was moving toward a doorway to the north. "Is that it?"

The large double doors were pulled open.

"Why are the doors so big?" I asked, confused. "I mean, look at those suckers. It has to be at least ten feet tall and each of those babies must weigh a ton."

"Piano nobile," Jillian reminded me. "This villa has a larger than normal first floor. That's why the windows and doors are so tall."

"Got it. Well, what do we have here? Not much to see in here. This must be one of the rooms that had a lot of problems. There's no furniture in here."

Jillian nodded. She gestured at the eastern wall, which had been stripped down to the framing.

"This room had more electrical problems than any of the others. I wish I knew what went on in here that caused so many problems."

"Fried the wiring, huh? Makes me wonder, too."

"I think you'll like the kitchen," Jillian told me, as we headed through the open doorway on the same wall.

"I can see most of it already," I chuckled, as I looked through the bare wall into the room next door. "Doesn't look very big, though."

"That's because what you're looking at isn't the kitchen. I think it's the pantry."

"The pantry is located off the dining room? Why wouldn't it be off the kitchen?"

"It *is* located off the kitchen. It's a pass-through pantry."

"Weird," I decided.

Jillian shook her head. "Not if you think about it. This place was large. There would have been servants. They walked through the pantry to deliver food there, in the dining room. Otherwise, they'd have to go back out, through Staircase Hall, through the living room, and then into the dining room."

"Hey, if it works, it works."

"Since this is going to be a bed and breakfast, I think I'll leave that as it is."

As we walked through the extensive kitchen, Jillian began detailing her plans on what she was going to do.

"Brand new appliances," she was saying. "Sub-zero fridge, six-burner stove, and a double wall oven. They'll go along this wall, here. Oh, and right here … I'm going to have a large island installed, complete with a sink, and maybe a couple of wine coolers."

I nodded. "Nice touch. I'd even make the island include a breakfast bar. It'd be a nice, informal place to grab a bite to eat."

Jillian nodded, opened the notebook she was still holding, and jotted my idea down.

"Did you see that this keeps going through here?" I asked, as I stepped through a doorway on the eastern side of the kitchen. "Now, what would you call this area? Ordinarily, I'd call it a pantry, but good grief. There's a window in here. This place doesn't have a second pantry, does it?"

Jillian thought for a moment and then shook her head, sending her long, curly brown hair tumbling about.

"Do you know what I think it is? I'll bet it's a 'servants only' area. There's enough room here for a normal dining table, with space for six chairs, I'd say."

"Like a break room for the servants," I decided.

"Exactly."

"This place is something else," I observed, with a smile.

"Do you like it?" Jillian hopefully asked.

"I do. I can't wait to see what you're going to do with it."

We explored the rest of the ground floor, but didn't find anything that looked as though it didn't belong. No missing locking pins for the scaffolding, no signs of wild animals, and certainly no signs of squatters. Then again, if squatters *were* hiding in this house, evidence would more than likely be found in one of the many rooms upstairs.

And, as long as we're talking about looking for evidence, no, I didn't find anything that suggested ghosts. I was kind of expecting to find maybe some hidden trip wires, or maybe a concealed speaker or two. However, the only thing I found was dust. Lots and lots of dust.

"Let me ask you something," I said, after a few minutes of silence had passed. "What *did* you do with all the existing furniture?"

"Yes. It's all in storage. I rented the largest unit they could give me. I've also told them to let me know when any other large units become available. Something tells me that I'll be needing at least one or two more of the units before this is all over."

I looked down at Sherlock. He was currently sitting on his butt and looking extremely content. A quick glance at Watson showed that she, too, seemed to be okay with this place. Neither of the dogs were showing any types of anxiety.

Jillian saw me looking at the dogs and squatted down next to Watson. She began caressing her silky red and white fur, which earned her several soft licks.

"I wonder if the others have found anything," Jillian said, as her hand moved to Watson's belly. The timid little corgi immediately rolled onto her back for better access. "How much longer should we give them?"

I shrugged. "Good question. I don't hear anything up there. For that matter, I don't hear anything below us, either. They certainly built these houses to last back then, didn't they?"

"That they did. Come on, Zachary. Let's go upstairs."

Both dogs were on their feet in a flash. I was practically yanked up the stairs as Sherlock raced up the curved wooden staircase. Jillian, holding Watson's leash, calmly took the stairs as though they were savoring each step. It was actually a good thing. I had managed to reclaim most of my breath by the time the two of them joined us on the second floor.

"Did you enjoy that sprint up the stairs?" Jillian wryly asked.

I shot a dark look at Sherlock before turning to my girlfriend.

"Not really. I think I pulled something by the seventh or eighth step."

"You silly man," Jillian teased. "Hmm, which way should we go?"

We were standing in a second Staircase Hall. Hallways and doors were everywhere, in all directions. My natural instincts told me I should go right, which is why I flat-out ignored them. Anyone who knows me will know I have the *worst* sense of direction.

"Do you hear anything?" I asked.

Jillian shook her head, but before she could say anything, both corgis turned left and pulled us through open double doors.

"I think this is the master bedroom," Jillian told me, as we stepped inside the large chamber. She pointed at the door directly ahead of us. "I absolutely love the terraces that these villas have. It's like this room has its own little patio. Isn't it gorgeous?"

Victorian Italianate villas were known for having a nice long list of things I've never heard of. Allow me to name just a few, to prove my point. There were corbels, which were mentioned earlier. They are, by definition, a structural piece of stone, wood, or metal which juts from a wall to carry a superincumbent weight. For the record, this house has a number of them.

Next, we have pedimented windows with architraves and archivolts. What that means is, you'll find a beam resting on the tops of columns. As for archivolts? Well, if you look at the top portion of this house, you'll find a decorative molding or band following the curves on the underside of every single arch, of which there are many.

And last, but certainly not least, there are something called *quoins*. While Jillian was explaining this one to me,

I had to quietly look it up on my phone. I had no idea she knew so much about architecture. Quoins are those masonry blocks you see at the corner of a wall. Some provide structural support, and others are just there for aesthetic purposes. And yes, before you ask, or can wonder about it, this house had those, too.

Thank you, Wikipedia.

"I can see why you want to keep everything original," I told Jillian, as I strode over to a large, angled bay window. I opened the door and stepped out onto the small terrace. "This place has a great view. Look, you've got mountains on the left, forest straight ahead, and I think I can see part of Rascal River on the right."

"You're right," Jillian confirmed, as she joined me outside.

I heard a collar rattle and I immediately looked down at the leashes we were still holding. Both dogs were waiting for us inside the room, and both, I might add, were focused on something else entirely. Curious to see what had captured their attention, I headed back inside.

In the middle of the room was an antique four poster bed. Sure, it had seen better days, but if I knew my girlfriend, she had every intention on restoring it. On either side of the giant bed were two small end tables. Sherlock was sniffing around the one on the right.

"Is there something in there, pal?" I asked him.

Sherlock snorted and waited while I rifled through the contents of the two drawers. Nope. Nothing there. Well, there were little bits of junk and trash, but nothing significant. Sherlock, however, was still staring at the small piece of furniture, so I dropped to all fours and peered under it. Still nothing.

"I don't know what you smell, but there isn't anything

here," I told the inquisitive corgi.

Both of the dogs looked east. My eyebrows shot up with surprise. Encompassing the entire eastern wall was what looked like a large, wooden carving. Stretching from floor to ceiling, it contained a wide variety of different pictures. I saw a castle, trees, and so on.

"That must've taken a long time to carve," I decided.

"It's a bas-relief!" Jillian exclaimed. She looked at my vacant expression and smiled. "It's a relief sculpture. It means the figures and objects are slightly raised from the background. Look at the size of it! I may not split this room in two after all. If I did, then that carving would have to go. It'd just be too dark. But, left alone, there's plenty of light. That alone is worth keeping this room as it is."

Both dogs wandered over to the giant carving, sniffed it a few times, and then looked up at me. I gave the leashes a gentle tug, indicating we had more to explore. The corgis snorted, resisted, and when it became clear we weren't staying to further study it, headed toward the opposite end of the room. Sherlock and Watson then looked north, at one of two doors facing us. Giving the corgi some extra slack, Sherlock pulled me over to the door on the right. I looked in and saw that it was a closet. At first glance, it looked deceptively small. That is, until you noticed the closet made a hard left turn and continued on. I don't think I had ever been in a closet in the shape of an 'L' before.

"You've got some storage space in here," I observed. "This must be what you were referring to when you suggested you could split the master bedroom up into two smaller bedrooms, right?"

Jillian nodded. "Right. I just don't think it'll happen now."

"Wow. Check out the duds. Think any of these can be saved?"

We were looking at a rack of long, ornate gowns. Then, on the rack next to it was another assortment of dresses, only they were clearly from another time. These were shorter, low-waisted dresses that looked as though they'd be revealing a lot of skin.

We were looking at Dame Highland's personal wardrobe.

As I flipped through the skimpy attire, I started to imagine what life must have been like back in the Roaring Twenties. Women exhibited their independence by listening to jazz music. They wore short skirts, bobbed their hair, and flaunted their disdain of anything that was considered socially acceptable.

"I cannot wait to go through these," Jillian said, as she smiled at me.

Just then, we heard a noise coming from back outside the room. Pulling the dogs away from the closet, we headed to the second Staircase Hall. Harry and Julie were just coming out of a door on the far southeastern corner of the hall.

"Hi, guys!" Julie cheerfully said, as she caught sight of us. "Find anything on the ground floor?"

"Nothing too remarkable," I reported. "How about you? What was in there?"

"It's just another room, man," Harry told us. "This house is huge. Personally, I don't see how people are going to get any sleep in here. This house creaks and groans all the time. It'd keep me awake at night, that's for sure."

"This house is old," I reminded Harry. "A little creaking and groaning is to be expected."

"Whatever, man. No offense, Jillian, but you won't catch me staying here. Ever."

"That's okay, Harry," Jillian said, keeping her face remarkably smile-free. "Staying at a B&B isn't for everyone. Have you checked all the doors yet?"

"Every time we go through a door, we find another room," Julie explained.

"How many have you checked so far?" Jillian wanted to know.

"This one makes five," Julie answered.

Jillian nodded. "Then that means there should be only one more. We were just in that one over there."

"The master bedroom," Julie said, nodding. "I liked that room. I loved the clothes in the closet. And speaking about love, I love that little patio in there."

"Isn't it cute?" Jillian gushed.

While the two women compared notes, Harry sidled closer to me.

"Tell me your honest opinion," Harry said. "What's your take on this place, man? Do you like it?"

I sighed and looked around the second story. I could very easily see this place bustling with paying customers. Jillian was sitting on a veritable gold mine.

"I think Jillian is one savvy businesswoman," I answered. "This place is gonna do amazingly well."

"No, not that. The ghost, man. Have you seen anything from her yet?"

I shook my head. "Are you serious? No. I mean, do you expect to see something?"

Harry was shaking his head.

"What do you think, man?" he whispered to me. "We're in *her* house, poking through *her* stuff. Don't you think you'd be teed off if someone did that to you in your own house?"

"You're really freaked out by this, aren't you?" I observed.

"What? Me? Of course not."

"There's no such thing as ghosts, pal."

"Says you. Mark my words. This place will make a believer out of you."

"Mm-hmm. Have you finished looking around up here?"

"There's one more room over here," Julie called, overhearing my question.

"Get to it, amigo," I said. "Jillian and I will be downstairs, okay? Oh, and if you see anything, scream like a little girl. I'll send Sherlock up to protect you."

"Bite me, man."

"What was that all about?" Jillian asked, as we headed back down the stairs.

"Julie and Harry are going to check the last room. I told Harry to scream like a little girl should he encounter a ghost. If I haven't died laughing, then I'll send Sherlock up."

"You're mean," Jillian observed.

I should point out here that she *did* smile at me.

A few minutes later, we both heard just that: a blood-curdling scream, but it didn't come from upstairs. This time, it came from somewhere behind us. Had Vance pulled another prank? Surely, my friend, the detective, wasn't stupid enough to prank his wife two times on the same day, was he?

The door on the immediate right of the staircase opened, and Tori appeared. She hadn't taken more than a few steps toward us when Vance appeared a split second later. I studied both of their faces, to see if I could determine what had happened. Tori appeared out of breath, while Vance had a wild-eyed expression on his face. And, oddly enough, he was seen tucking his shirt back into place, as though it had been forcefully yanked up. What that could possibly mean, I didn't know. I could only figure Vance had just booked himself a month-long stay at Doghouse Central.

"That..." Vance stammered. "That *sooo* wasn't cool, Tori."

Tori took one look at Jillian and burst out laughing. Comprehension dawned. Vance hadn't pulled a prank on Tori, but the other way around. From the sounds of things, Tori had just settled the score with her joke-loving husband.

"What's the matter there, buddy? You look like you've seen a ghost."

Jillian and Tori both giggled, while Vance shot me as dark of a look as he could muster.

"I had better not find out this was your idea," he began. "If it was, then ... then..."

"Then what?" I asked, after the girls had stopped laughing. "For the record, I had nothing to do with whatever happened down there. And, I will admit, I'm curious. What *did* happen?"

"Would you like to tell him, or should I?" Tori wheezed out, between laughs.

Vance grumbled something unintelligible and crossed his arms over his chest.

"Me it is. So, Captain Courageous here was poking through a few boxes we found down in the basement, and just so you know, I don't think I've ever seen a basement that big. It's like a third story. Anyway, my dear old husband had his back to me, and just then, I saw a bug running along the ground."

Jillian clapped a hand over her mouth.

"You didn't."

"I most certainly did," Tori said, as a wicked smile formed on her face. "I snatched that nasty little sucker up and dropped it down the back of Vance's shirt. You would have thought that he had just sat on an ant hill. Oh, I only wish I had recorded that. It would have been the second video on YouTube that went viral."

We all heard footsteps on the staircase and looked up. Harry and Julie must have finished their inspection of the second floor. Or else they heard the commotion and were curious. Probably both.

"What happened down here?" Harry wanted to know. "We could hear the screams all the way up there. Tori, are you okay? Vance, not cool, bro. I can't believe you'd try to punk your wife again."

Vance pointed a finger at me and Jillian.

"How do you know it wasn't one of those two?"

"Please," Harry scoffed. "Zack would never pull something like that. He never did in high school, and I can't imagine him starting now."

"True story," I admitted, with a shrug.

"I wasn't the one screaming," Tori said, which drew another scowl from Vance.

Harry stared incredulously at Vance.

"Dude, that was *you*? Man, you sounded like a 12-year-old girl!"

"Kiss my ass," Vance growled.

"What happened?" Julie wanted to know.

"Tori dropped a live bug down Vance's shirt," Jillian

said, between giggles. "I can only figure he thought it was a spider. What was it, anyway?"

Tori shrugged. "It wasn't a spider. Maybe some type of beetle? Now that I think about it, it could've been a cockroach."

"Call an exterminator," Jillian quietly noted to herself, as she set a reminder on her phone.

"You're afraid of bugs?" Harry continued.

"Absolutely not," Vance argued. "I'm just not expecting to find any inside my shirt, thank you very much."

"Behave yourself and perhaps there won't be another time," Tori admonished.

"Did you find anything down there?" I wanted to know. I was anxious to change the subject because I could see the look that had appeared on Vance's face. He was embarrassed and very close to having a full-fledged argument with Tori. Personally, I didn't want to be a witness to that. "And no, I'm not talking about ghost stuff. Find anything cool?"

Vance turned to look at me. His face finally softened and he smiled. He nodded.

"As a matter of fact, we did. We found a pool table hiding under a tarp. It's in really good condition. I might try to buy that off of you, Jillian, only I'll need to buy new balls."

The entire room fell silent.

Vance's face flamed up, "Now wait a minute. That's not what I meant. Those balls were pink and I don't want to play with pink balls."

No one moved a muscle, nor uttered a peep.

"Billiard balls, for crying out loud. Would you guys get your minds out of the gutter?"

The girls shared a look together at the exact same time

both Harry and I snorted with amusement.

"And where would you put a pool table?" Tori asked, bewildered. "We're short on room as it is."

"Vance, I'd like to see this table," Jillian said. "Will you show it to me?"

We followed Vance and Tori as they retraced their steps to the basement. Tori was right. The basement was huge! Judging from the looks of it, there was just as much square footage as the other two floors. Talk about having your own private storage facility!

"You can find it right over there," Vance said, pointing at a large, flat object covered by a yellowing tarp.

I pulled the musty tarp back to reveal a somewhat dusty walnut table with a surprisingly blemish-free playing field made of an olive green felt. I then noticed the table had eight legs, and each leg was hexagonal by design. Noticing something that was off, I studied the table for a few moments before I realized what it was. The size.

This table was closer to the ground than any pool table I had ever seen. I would have guessed that it was less than three feet tall. It also looked larger. I looked over at Jillian and saw that she had her phone in her hand and was busy tapping something on the screen. After a few moments, her face lit up with a smile and she showed me her phone.

"It's a snooker table! Do you see the smaller pockets? And that there are only six of them?"

"I'll be damned," Vance muttered. "I didn't even pick up on that."

"Snooker?" I quizzically repeated. "What's that?"

"It's played on a larger table than pool," Jillian explained, as she read from her phone. "You use fifteen pink numberless balls, six numbered object balls, and the cue balls."

"I told you they were pink," Vance haughtily informed us.

The room fell silent again. Harry snorted, and received a thump in the gut from Julie.

"I didn't know anyone played snooker anymore," Tori said.

"I don't think they do," I added.

"I'm sorry, Vance," Jillian said, as she gazed fondly down at the table, "but I'm afraid the snooker table isn't for sale. This is just the sort of thing I want upstairs, in the house. Think of it as another way to bring back a little piece of the past."

"Look at all the boxes in here," I said, as I looked around the vast area. "Did you go through any of them?"

"Just a few," Tori admitted. "I didn't want to get too nosey. These things all belong to Jillian now."

"I really don't mind," Jillian assured her friend. "So, what did you find?"

"That one over there had some old drinking glasses. And that one? The one closest to you, Zack. It had a couple of photo albums in it."

Jillian perked up.

"Photo albums? In that one? Zachary, would you pass them to me, please?"

"Sure."

I opened the fragile, crumbling box and saw the albums in question. After handing them to Jillian, I pointed upstairs.

"Let's head back up. I think we've kicked up too much dust down here."

Right on cue, I heard Sherlock snort. I looked down

just as both dogs looked up. Each corgi was sporting a fine film of dust on their shiny coats. And, Sherlock had several smudges on his face, as though he had found something interesting on the ground and had shoved his entire snout in it, as he was wont to do.

"Come on, you two. I think we could all use some fresh air."

As we relaxed up in the living room, comparing notes about what we had found, I couldn't help but notice that not one person said anything about the existence of ghosts. Aside from Vance's prank with the spooky sound effects and Tori's retaliatory insect attack, it had been a spook-free night. A small part of me was disappointed, in that I was hoping some type of supernatural presence would have made their presence known, even though I'm sure it would have scared the bejeesus out of me.

I was about ready to park my butt on the closest flat surface, being anxious to give my tiring feet a break, when Sherlock tugged on his leash. Curious, I looked down at him, but he only had eyes for Jillian. Right about then, I noticed Jillian wasn't talking, but staring, open-mouthed, at one of the photo albums we had brought back from the basement. I also noticed her phone was in her other hand.

"What is it?" I asked.

Jillian didn't respond.

"Hey, are you okay over there?" I asked, raising my voice a little so that I knew she'd be able to hear me.

She finally looked my way. Her astonished eyes met mine and then she held up the photo album.

"I … I think I know why Dame Highland was murdered."

"Why?" I asked, as I rose to my feet. I promptly leaned

over Jillian's shoulder to look at the picture that had caught her attention. "Is this her? Dame Highland?"

Jillian nodded. "Yes."

"Looks like she's wearing one of those outfits we saw in the closet," I observed. "One of the, uh, racier ones."

"Look at her," Vance argued. "If you've got it, flaunt it. She's got the body for it. She was definitely a looker, that's for … but you know what? No one cares about what she looked like. I sure don't."

"Nice save, genius," Tori quipped, as she gave her husband a scowl.

Everyone crowded around the picture. There, sitting in a shiny old-fashioned roadster, waving enthusiastically at the photographer, was a young woman who must have been in her twenties. She was slim, had short dark hair, and was wearing a slinky, off the shoulder dress with a dark cloche hat.

"Do you see it yet?" Jillian anxiously asked. "Have you spotted it?"

I was about ready to tell her that I hadn't a clue what she was talking about when I noticed Vance's eyes widen with surprise. He leaned closer, presumably for a better look. Then his shocked eyes found Jillian's.

"Is that what I think it is?"

"We can't be certain its authentic," Jillian excitedly began, "but I'm pretty sure we'll find out that it is."

"What am I looking at?" I asked again, growing frustrated.

Thankfully, I wasn't the only one who hadn't spotted whatever Jillian was trying to show us. Harry and Julie looked just as puzzled as I felt, and Tori? She … nope, there she goes. I could tell she had just spotted the same thing Vance had.

"Oh, this changes everything," Tori told her friend.

FIVE

The following day, by noon, we were hundreds of miles away from Pomme Valley. Why? Allow me to explain. That picture from last night? The one of Dame Highland, in her car? Well, as you know, Jillian had spotted something remarkable in the photo—which Vance had confirmed—and *that* was the reason why we were currently in the middle of a 7-hour road trip. What was it she had noticed? Well, let me take you back to last night, when the photo's significance had to be explained to me.

"Do you see this here, Zachary?" Jillian had asked me, as she came up beside me to point at Dame Highland.

"It's our ghost, but in pre-ghost form," I joked.

"Do you see what she's wearing?"

"Looks like a dress. I can't see all of it, 'cause she's

leaning out of her car's window. Are you talking about the hat? I've seen them before. I know it's bell-shaped, and probably has a proper name for it, but I don't know what it is."

"It's a cloche hat," Jillian explained.

"Right. She's wearing a cloche hat. What about it?"

"What else do you see?"

I held the picture closer to my face.

"Well, she has on a few pieces of jewelry."

"Right! Exactly."

"I wouldn't say it's anything to get excited about. They're just rings."

Jillian's elation slowly evaporated. She leaned forward to tap a point on Dame Highland's neck.

"No, this here. Do you see this?"

"Looks like a brooch, I guess. Isn't that what typically holds a cloak together?"

"You think she's wearing a cloak?"

"Well, no, but obviously the style of clothes back then might have had something similar. Besides, isn't she wearing something over her shoulders?"

"That's a shawl," Jillian corrected.

I squinted at the photograph.

"All right. So, we're talking about this brooch-which-isn't-a-brooch. What about it?"

"A brooch is a large pin that is typically worn on a winter coat. No, this is being worn, like a necklace. Do you see it now?"

Vance, being the schmuck that he was, produced a magnifying glass and, with a huge grin on his face, offered it to me. I shot him a dark look, but no one was paying attention. Jillian took the magnifier and held it over the photograph. Then she pointed at the junction of the shawl, which happened to fall on the base of Ms. Highland's neck. And ... that's when I saw it.

"If this isn't a brooch, then what is it? It looks like a big jewel."

Jillian nodded excitedly, "It is! I did a quick search online and found an obscure reference to something so bizarre and rare that it needs confirmation."

"What? What do you think that is? Is it really a jewel?"

"I think so."

"What kind?"

Jillian shrugged. "I don't know. That's what I'm hoping to find out. Typically, jewels that large have names."

"And how are you going to identify a piece of jewelry from an old photograph?"

"We found out a relative of hers is still living," Jillian reminded me. "A niece, I think."

"And this niece is going to be able to identify that?" I asked, incredulous.

"Let's find out together, shall we? What do you say to a road trip?"

Now, let's return to our regularly scheduled programming.

Here we are, speeding north, in an attempt to track down a living relative who may—or may not—be able to tell us what Dame Highland was wearing in the picture. I can only assume that this jewel, if that's what it really was, had to be at least several hundred carats in size. I had to admit, a jewel that large would probably be worth a pretty penny. What I wanted to know was, what type of stone was it? I didn't think it was a diamond, since the photo showed the gem wasn't clear. True, the photo was black and white, and determining the exact color would be impossible. However, we could also tell that it was a darker color. Maybe a sapphire? Emerald?

Curious, I performed several quick searches on the Internet. There simply weren't any recorded precious stones that were that size and shape which were known to exist in that time frame. Of the ones I did find, and were roughly the same size, I could only drool. We're talking about jewels worth millions of dollars. Was Jillian right? Could this be what Dame Highland was murdered over? Could someone have found out that she was in possession of some priceless piece of jewelry, and *that* was why she had been attacked and—presumably—tortured to death? And, if all the above happened to be true, and seeing how none of Dame Highland's jewelry had ever been found, did that mean there's a chance this mystery jewel could still be somewhere on the property?

I returned my attention to the road. Yes, that had to be exactly what Jillian was thinking. Why else would she want to make a long road trip in the middle of the week? And, for Pete's sake, why didn't this relative have a computer? The ability to scan a picture and electronically attach it to an email had to be the easiest way to transfer a photo from one end of the country to the other. Plus, it could be done in the blink of an eye. However, did Ms. Katherine O'Connor own a computer? Did any of her friends?

No.

"Penny for your thoughts?"

I looked over at Jillian and sighed. "I was just thinking how much time we could've saved if Ms. O'Connor would have had a computer."

She shrugged. "It's unthinkable for me and you.

However, if you didn't grow up with one, or else have a need to use one, then there's no reason to purchase one."

"There's always a reason to need one," I argued. "Hey, do we know how old this Katherine lady is? I mean, if her aunt lived in the Roaring Twenties and died sometime in the '40s, then how old do you think she is? It's not possible, is it?"

"She could have been born in the '30s," Jillian informed me. "I have a great aunt who was born in 1929. I still get Christmas cards from her every year. She's just as spry as she ever was, and she just turned 90."

"Incredible," I breathed.

"What I wouldn't give to be able to see what life was like in the '20s," Jillian said, in a wistful tone.

I shrugged. "We're talking about being back in the time of gangsters and Prohibition, right?"

Jillian nodded. "That's right. Women were expected to conduct themselves primly and properly, and if they didn't, they were publicly ridiculed. They would bring shame to themselves and their families if they didn't cover up and behave accordingly."

"Then what about Dame Highland?" I asked. "We both saw that picture of her. She didn't look like she was trying to cover anything up. In fact, quite the opposite. I'd say she was rebelling."

Jillian smiled. "I think that was *exactly* what she was doing. They had a term for girls like that."

"Slutty?" I guessed.

Jillian laughed and smacked my arm.

"No, of course not. The term is *flappers*. Dame Highland was obviously a flapper girl."

"A flapper girl? I've never heard that term before. So,

tell me. What makes someone classify a girl as a flapper?"

"Flapper girls were known for their proclivity to dance to jazz music. They wore shorter skirts and slinkier outfits, which made it easier for them to dance. Those girls smoked, oftentimes spoke in their own language, and truly lived in the moment."

"How do you know so much about this subject?" I asked, perplexed.

"You'll find me well versed in many subjects," Jillian admitted, as she smiled at me. "Once I realized that Highland House's former owner was more than likely a flapper girl, I took it upon myself to learn everything I could about the period. Zachary, that period of time was fascinating, to say the least. Those girls embraced anything society deemed immoral or dangerous. I believe those young ladies were the first generation of independent American women."

"You learn something new every day," I murmured.

"Indeed," Jillian agreed. "Flappers pushed barriers in economic, political, and sexual freedom. The 1920s were known for Prohibition. It … you know what that means, don't you?"

"Of course," I nodded. "The US Government bowed to the rising temperance movement and banned the production, importation, transportation, and sales of all alcoholic beverages."

"An apt definition," Jillian observed.

"I wrote a book based in that period of American History. I needed to sound like I knew what I was talking about, so I did my research."

"You did your research and didn't know what a flapper girl was?" Jillian teased. "Now, as I was saying, the 1920s were known for Prohibition. It started in 1920 and was in place up until 1933, with the ratification of the 21st Amendment, which essentially repealed the 18th Amendment."

"With you so far," I said.

"Good. Now, what many people don't realize is that women were entering the workforce during this time. Automobile factories sprang into existence, which drove prices down. It afforded young people more mobility."

"Okay, spill," I ordered. "How do you know so much about *this* subject?"

"Hey, I read," Jillian insisted.

"I do, too," I argued. "Even with all the research I did for my book, which was set in the 1920s, mind you, I didn't learn that much."

"Maybe you did and you just don't remember it?" Jillian suggested.

"My memory isn't that bad," I grumped.

"I'm just teasing you, Zachary. Very well. I'll be honest. I might have taken a class on the subject in college."

"And you remember that much about it?"

"Don't you remember all the classes you took while you were in college?" Jillian returned.

"Not like that, I don't."

Several hours later, we were driving across the Tacoma Narrows strait of the Puget Sound. The Tacoma Narrows Bridge is a pair of suspension bridges which connect the city of Tacoma with the Kitsap Peninsula. The original bridge, I later learned, collapsed four months after it opened to the public, in 1940. The replacement bridge, constructed ten years later, was the same one we were presently on. The addition of the second bridge, to relieve traffic congestion, didn't happen until 2007.

"I like this area," Jillian told me, as we exited the bridge onto the Kitsap Peninsula. "I love the greenery here."

"Like Oregon, this place gets lots of rain."

"Let me guess. You wrote a book which required you to research the Puget Sound?"

"Kinda. Several characters in my third book originated from Federal Way, which is about halfway between Tacoma and Seattle. So yeah, I've done some research on this area, too."

We found the assisted living facility where Katherine O'Connor was living nearly thirty minutes later. The complex was huge, had acres of green grass everywhere, and from the number of elderly seniors sitting on benches, or playing cards on tables, it must have been a favorite among retired people. Jillian tapped me on the shoulder and pointed at a Visitor's Parking area on my left.

"I sure do hope she remembers something that'll help us," I said five minutes later, as I set both dogs down on the ground. I handed Watson's purple leash to Jillian as I wrapped Sherlock's green one tightly around my hand. We were in another state, and the last thing I wanted to worry about was playing *Chase the Corgi* over unfamiliar terrain.

"We can only hope and see. Now, let's see about checking in and finding out where we can find Katherine."

It turns out that assisted living centers absolutely love it when dogs visit their facilities. Why? Because seniors have a tendency to light up and become more interactive when a dog is present. Make it two dogs, who absolutely adored the extra attention, and you'll quickly become the hit of the facility. We were stopped every ten feet by someone anxious to offer both of the dogs a friendly pat on the head.

"Can someone tell us where … do you know how we can find section 9? No? Umm, how about you? Could you point us to … okay, I give up. No one is paying attention to us."

Jillian offered me a smile.

"That's probably because you're not talking very loud, and just about everyone here is probably wearing a hearing aid."

A young man wearing navy blue scrubs suddenly rounded the corner. He was holding several clipboards and was humming merrily to himself. Deciding this was our best chance of finding Ms. O'Connor's room, I held up a hand as I stepped out in front of the guy.

"Yes? Can I help you?"

"I certainly hope so. We're looking for room #131. We were told it was in section 9. Are we close?"

"Room #131?" the orderly slowly repeated. "That's Ms. O'Connor's room. Can I ask you what this is in regards to?" The young man's gaze dropped to the ground and he spotted Sherlock and Watson. "Oh! Have you come to cheer up Ms. O'Connor? She's been depressed these last few weeks. I had long ago given up hope that she'd have any more visitors before she passes."

"Has her health been deteriorating?" Jillian asked, worriedly.

The orderly shrugged. "It certainly looks that way. Although, I'd like to say for the record, once the patient gives up, so to speak, then I don't think they'll be around too much longer. As for Ms. O'Connor, I think she's lost her will to live."

"That's sad," I observed.

"Are you friends or family?" the orderly asked.

"Friends," Jillian answered.

The orderly nodded. "Good. Very well, you'll find her down at the end of that hallway. It'll be the last door on the left."

"Ms. O'Connor?" Jillian quietly asked, after we knocked on the open door a few times, but didn't hear any response. "Are you here?"

I was about ready to poke my head into the room when I heard Sherlock whine. I had just looked down at him, anxious to keep him quiet, when I made the mistake of passing his leash from one hand to the other. Sure enough, Sherlock was waiting.

"Hey! What are you doing?" I angrily hissed at Sherlock, as he went trotting into the room. "Get back here!"

If I didn't know any better, then I'd say that little booger *strutted* into the room. The inquisitive corgi quickly located the room's occupant (she was asleep in her rocking chair) and reared up so he could put his two stumpy front legs on her lap. This, of course, immediately woke her up.

"My, my. What have we here?"

Sherlock whined and yipped exasperatingly, as though he was trying to say no one naps without his permission.

"I'm so sorry, Ms. O'Connor," I began, as I hurried into the room and snatched the fallen leash off the ground. "Sherlock got away from me. I hope he didn't disturb you."

"Oh, balderdash," the old woman responded, as she dismissed my concerns. She laid a frail, wrinkled hand on Sherlock's head and gave the corgi a surprisingly thorough scratching behind his ears. The room's occupant finally looked up at me and she smiled. "Am I to assume this cute little furball is yours?"

Watson yipped excitedly from her position by Jillian's side.

"And what's this? There's a second one! Well, come here, you adorable fluffball. I'd like to say hello to you, too."

Watson practically *flung* herself away from Jillian's side and rushed into the room. She slid to a stop several feet from Katherine's rocker and wriggled with delight. Within moments, both corgis were jostling about as each competed with the other to get as much attention from the stranger as possible.

"Would you two behave yourself?" I scolded, as I leaned down to pick up Watson's leash. "Man alive, you'd think I kept them kenneled all day and never gave them any attention whatsoever."

Katherine's eyes returned to mine.

"And who might you be, young man?"

I held out a hand. After a few moments, Katherine placed her frail hand in mine.

"Katherine O'Connor? I'm Zachary Anderson. This is Jillian Cooper. Sherlock is on your right, and Watson is on your left. I hope you don't mind, but we'd like to know if we can sit with you for a bit and ask you some questions about a relative of yours."

"Stories? You'd like to sit with me and listen to my stories? Heavens above, it's what I do best. Pull up a chair, both of you."

Bemused, I retrieved two chairs from the other side of the room and positioned them close to Katherine's chair.

"What would you like me to tell you?" Katherine began, as she looked first at me, and then at Jillian.

"You're not what I expected," I began.

Katherine's sharp eyes focused on mine.

"You were expecting, what, a dull, glazed over

expression to be on my face? Maybe have a lap full of knitting?"

I grinned sheepishly and shrugged.

"Well, you're only half right," the elderly senior admitted, with a chuckle. "My knitting is over there, on the bed. I can only knit for so long each day before I become tempted to gouge my eyes out with my needles."

I couldn't help it. I snorted with laughter. Yep, complete with porcine sound effects. Katherine's eyes sparkled with amusement.

"Pardon me, dear. I guess that wasn't too grandmotherly of me, was it?"

"My grandmother never sounded like that," I chortled. "You certainly don't sound like a, uh, er…"

"Like what?" Katherine innocently asked. "An old fart? A decrepit geezer?"

I heard a titter of laughter from Jillian. She was trying her hardest not to laugh, too, and was having just as much success as I was. I grinned at the elderly woman. I liked her!

"It's okay, dear. When you reach my age, about the only thing left that still works worth a hoot is my mind. You say you want to ask me about a relative? I have none left, I'm afraid. Therefore, you either have the wrong person, or else you want to talk about someone who has passed?"

I nodded. "I'm sorry to say that this person *did* die a long time ago."

Katherine's face fell.

"Oh, dear. Just when I was beginning to like the two of you."

"I'm sorry?" I asked, confused.

"Young man, you're here for one reason, and one reason only. You want to know about Aunt Hilda, don't you?"

I shook my head. "Aunt Hilda? Never heard of her. I, er, *we* were hoping to talk to you about Dame Highland."

Katherine looked over at Jillian and gave her a bewildered look. Jillian smiled, placed a hand over Katherine's, and then placed her other hand over mine.

"Zachary, she *is* talking about Dame Highland. Hilda was her first name."

"Oh. Sorry."

"I should have known you two would be asking about her. Everyone has, at some point in time."

"Why's that?" I asked, genuinely curious.

"Young man, don't take me for a fool. You're looking for my late aunt's jewelry. Don't deny it."

"Believe it or not, I'm not," I insisted.

"I just purchased Highland House," Jillian said, drawing a gasp from the old woman. "I'm not interested in her jewelry, either. What I *am* interested in is trying to get the house fully restored. Now, there seems to be some debate on whether or not the house is cursed..."

"...or haunted," I added.

"Several of the workers I've hired to do the renovation have become injured. One has even died."

"And you want to know whether or not Aunt Hilda is responsible?" Katherine incredulously asked. "Dear, I may be old, but I'm not senile. I do not believe in ghosts."

Jillian smiled. "Good for you. I don't, either. Now, the only thing I'm interested in is turning your aunt's house into a bed and breakfast."

"And the fact that hundreds of thousands of dollars' worth of jewelry are rumored to be hidden somewhere in that house means nothing to you?"

Jillian and I stared at each other. I'm sure my mouth fell open. Hundreds of thousands of dollars? Was she referring to the big jewel from the photo?

"I know this is going to be hard to believe," I slowly began, "but neither of us are interested in any old jewelry. She only wants to restore the house, and I only want what's best for her."

Jillian slipped her hand into mine.

"That's sweet. Thank you, Zachary."

I felt a flush forming.

"I do find that hard to believe," the elderly woman admitted. "I don't think you realize how many have searched for her missing jewelry over the years."

"Was her collection that extensive or did she only have a few pieces that were worth that much money?" I asked.

Katherine winked at me, "Both."

"How did she make her money?" Jillian suddenly asked. "Back then, it would have taken a lot of money to have a house like hers, cars, clothes, and a collection of jewelry as extensive as you say, wouldn't it?"

Katherine pointed at a nearby bookcase.

"Would you be a dear and hand me that photo album? The blue one that's thicker than the others?"

I spotted the requested album and gingerly pulled it off its shelf. It was thick, all right. It was crammed full of photos, newspaper clippings, and so on. I gently handed the book to Dame Hilda Highland's descendent.

"Would you stop treating me as though I'm made of lace?" Katherine demanded, as she plopped the album down on her lap. "Mercy, have you never met someone as old as I am before?"

"Er, how old are you?" I tentatively asked.

"Zachary!" Jillian quietly hissed. "You never ask a woman her age. Ever!"

"It's okay, dear," Katherine assured Jillian. The elderly woman turned back to me. "I'm 93. In seven years, then you can make a fuss. Provided I'm still around, of course."

"I'm sure you will be," I assured her. "In fact, Jillian and I would love to attend your 100th birthday party, provided we're invited."

Katherine looked down at the dogs, "Of course you're invited, dear. And so are your dogs. Now, let me get to answering your lovely wife's question."

"Oh, we're not married," I said.

Katherine looked first at me, then at Jillian. Within moments, she was nodding thoughtfully.

"What?" I asked. "What's that look for?"

"You may not be married yet, young Zachary, but you will be when you come back."

Surprised, I turned to Jillian, who smiled warmly at me.

"You two will make a fine couple." Katherine opened the album and carefully flipped a few pages. "Ah, here we are. Do you see this? This is one of the earliest photographs I have of Aunt Hilda."

"She was very beautiful," Jillian observed. "What was she here, twelve?"

"Let's see. That's my grandfather there, and he passed away before my mother finished school, and do you see the dog? That's Benny. I could never forget him. If Benny was still alive, then that means Hilda was thirteen or fourteen. Now, the reason I'm showing you this picture is to bring your attention to this. Do you see what's hanging on the wall behind Hilda?"

"Looks like a painting," Jillian decided.

"That's right. I later learned that particular painting was an actual Monet. The paintings were always changing in that house."

"Pardon me for asking," Jillian quietly began, "but were the paintings stolen?"

Katherine nodded. "I believe so. My grandparents were wealthy, but I don't think they earned their money honestly. Oh, here's the picture I wanted you to see. What would you say to this, Mr. Anderson?"

I leaned forward so that I could get a better look at the picture Katherine was tapping. From my upside-down vantage point, it looked like a matronly lady cooking something on a huge, antique gas stove. Well, I guess back then, those giant stoves were the norm.

"Is that your grandmother?" I asked. "And she's cooking something?"

"Heavens above," Katherine sighed. "You aren't that observant, are you?"

Jillian giggled softly.

"I'm talking about this here. Through this doorway? What can you see?"

"Crates," I reported. "Lots of crates, and they look like they're stacked all the way to the ceiling."

Katherine was nodding. "Exactly. Now, what do you think are in those crates?"

Jillian crossed her arms over her chest as she considered her answer.

"What was the year?"

Katherine peeled back the protective plastic covering the photo and peered at the back.

"1924."

"Right smack in the middle of Prohibition," Jillian softly mused. "It's booze. Alcohol. Something which had been deemed illegal to possess."

"That's right. Good for you, dear. Now, why do you think I showed you those two pictures?"

"Stolen paintings," I began, "and crates of booze. So, that's how the Highlands earned their money. Smuggling?"

"I'm afraid so," Katherine sighed, and leaned back in her chair.

I glanced down at the open album and spotted the photo on the opposite page. I immediately recognized Dame Highland. She and another woman, who looked to be the same age, were standing next to a slick, gleaming car that looked as though it could belong to Bugsy Malone.

I whistled appreciatively.

"She was a looker, wasn't she?" Katherine idly commented.

"Hmm? Oh, yeah, I guess so." I leaned forward to tap the picture of the car. "I was actually referring to this. That's a nice-looking car."

Katherine nodded knowingly, "Aunt Hilda's car. She told me she purchased that car on her 21st birthday. Aunt Hilda loved that car more than anything."

"What kind is it?" I asked, as I peered closely at the picture. "It doesn't look like a Ford. I mean, it's kinda shaped like a Model A, but it looks flatter. Stretched, even."

"It's not a Model A," Katherine confirmed. "She told me once what type it was, only … I'm sorry. I don't remember what it is. If I think of it, then I'll be sure to let you know."

"It's not important," Jillian assured the elderly woman. "Do you know the identity of the other woman?"

Katherine's eyes dropped to the album and she smiled.

"Why, that's my mother, of course. Penelope. She and Hilda were as close as sisters could be."

"That's sweet," Jillian softly murmured. "They look very happy together. From the looks of things, I'd say they were about to go out for a drive. They certainly looked as though they were enjoying life."

"And why wouldn't they?" Katherine countered, her voice becoming strong. "Aunt Hilda's businesses were booming. She was making money hand over fist. And yes, before you object, I know she wasn't making her money honestly, but that's in the past."

"No one is judging her," I assured the old woman.

Katherine patted my hand, "Good for you, dear. As I was saying, my aunt loved fine clothes, she loved her jewelry, and she loved to have a good time. Especially dancing. She was such a fine dancer." Katherine's expression darkened. "All good things must come to an end, I'm afraid. Aunt Hilda must have frequented the wrong speakeasy. Somehow, and I don't know if we'll ever figure out how, my aunt caught the eye of several degenerates. Oh, I'll never forget that day. Mother wasn't the same after Hilda was gone."

"Can you tell us what happened?" Jillian softly asked.

"It was August 17, 1947," Katherine began. "I had returned home from school to find my mother crying. When I asked her what was wrong, she could only tell me she was gone. I didn't learn she was talking about Aunt Hilda until several days later. Strangely enough, no one would talk to me. It's not like I was a child, for heaven's sake. I had to take it upon myself to find out what had happened."

"How old were you?" Jillian quietly asked.

"Fifteen."

"What did you find out?" I wanted to know.

"Well, two men had broken into Aunt Hilda's house

and ransacked it. They practically destroyed the interior of the house as they searched high and low. It was the jewelry, you see. Since they had been unsuccessful in locating her hidden stash of jewels, they turned their attention to my aunt. They…"

At this, the elderly woman choked up. She pulled a tissue from a nearby box and gently dabbed the corners of her eyes.

"They tortured my aunt mercilessly as they tried to get her to disclose where she had stashed her jewels. When the police found her, she was still alive, but she passed away several hours later at the hospital. The doctors said she had undergone extreme physical duress at the hands of those two men."

"I'm so sorry," Jillian all but whispered. Her eyes had filled. Without saying anything, Katherine reached for the tissue box and held one out to Jillian. "Thank you. No one deserved to be treated like that. At least they got what they deserved."

Katherine hesitated and looked up.

"Those thugs? They were captured? When? Where? How do you know this?"

"They were discovered a week later, in Medford," Jillian answered. "It's the only thing my realtor could tell me about what had happened to the previous owner of Highland House."

"They were caught that quickly? I'm glad. Wait. You said 'discovered'. Were they found dead?"

Jillian nodded. "Yes. As for how they knew, well, that was, er, because of the smell."

"What do you supposed happened to them?" Katherine asked as she first looked at Jillian, and then me.

Jillian helplessly shrugged and looked hopefully at me. I thought about the two dead men, and the fact that they were found together, and finally nodded.

"If I were to guess, then I'd say that they probably turned on the other. Are we certain no one found any of your aunt's jewelry?"

"It's what I was told," Katherine answered. "Unless someone tried to sell a piece or two, we will never know."

Jillian reached into her purse and pulled out the picture from last night. She held it out to Katherine, who hesitantly accepted it. Her wrinkled face lit up once her eyes focused on the photograph.

"Oh, my! I didn't think there were any pictures left of it."

I eagerly leaned forward and tapped the picture of Aunt Hilda.

"Is this a gem?"

Katherine frowned, "I thought you didn't care about her jewelry, young man."

"I still don't care about it," I insisted. I put a protective arm around Jillian's shoulders. "I care about her and her ability to stay safe."

"Can you tell us about this?" Jillian hopefully asked.

Katherine's face became grim and her lips thinned.

"Please?" Jillian continued. "Is this why Hilda was killed?"

Katherine finally nodded, and her answer came out in a strained whisper, "Yes."

"All for a darned necklace," I grumbled.

The look Katherine gave me suggested she believed I wasn't playing with a full deck.

"What?" I asked, growing defensive.

"*That*, dear boy, is the *Czarina's Tear*."

"It has a name?" I skeptically asked.

"All famous gems do," Katherine informed me.

It was at this time, Jillian confided later, that she had taken a few steps back and Googled the gem. In the meantime, I was still reluctant to believe a simple jewel would have a name like *Czarina's Tear*, and an unremarkable one at that. That's when I heard Katherine sigh.

"Very well, dear. You have me convinced. You don't care about the stone."

"Not at all," I confirmed. "So, it has a name. Big deal. That still doesn't tell us anything about it."

"It's a demantoid garnet," Jillian announced.

"It's a demon *what*?" I asked, certain I had heard that wrong. "And how did you learn that?"

"A demantoid garnet," Jillian repeated. "And I looked it up."

I shrugged. "A garnet. Okay. Well, those aren't worth as much as diamonds, but I guess it's still considered a semi-precious stone. What else do you know about it?"

"It's 504 carats in size."

I thought back to what I knew about gemstones and their respective sizes. I was pretty sure a one-carat diamond typically retailed for around $4,000 to $5,000, and that was for a decent quality stone. Nice stones could retail for twice that. This garnet was over 500 carats? I was shocked to discover my mouth had become bone dry.

"That's, um, big, isn't it?"

"Men," Katherine scoffed. "You don't appreciate the finer things in life, do you? Yes, it's big. I saw it once. It was the size of a chicken egg."

"A 500-carat garnet," I mused. "Wow. That's gotta be

worth something to someone."

Jillian, who was still reading about the gemstone on her phone, suddenly grasped my arm. Tightly.

"Zachary, it says here that the largest known demantoid garnet is around 200 carats. This one is more than twice that! Do you know what that means? That stone must be priceless!"

SIX

"What do you think?" I asked Jillian. It was Sunday, the day before Robert, Jillian's foreman, had told us that he'd find another crew and be back to work. "Do you really think this *Czarina's Tear* thingamajig could be hidden somewhere in this house?"

"She died in 1947," Jillian reminded me. "The realtor told me the house sat vacant for all those years. If that gem *was* in here somewhere, then it would have been found long ago. I can't even begin to imagine how many people probably searched this house upon learning it was vacant. No wonder Hilda's ghost is roaming the halls."

"Not funny," I scolded, as I turned to look at her. "And you don't fool me. I know you don't believe in ghosts. You've said so yourself, on many occasions."

"True," Jillian admitted. She shrugged and let her purse slide off her shoulder and down her arm. She caught the purse before it could fall to the floor and placed it on a table just inside the foyer. "Lock the door, would you?"

"Already did," I assured her. I looked down at the dogs. Both were staring at me as though they couldn't believe we were back here. "Don't look at me like that. We're going to take a closer look at things, okay? You guys might've missed something the first time around. Jillian? How would you like to start? What are we looking for this time?"

"I really don't know, Zachary. Your dogs have a knack for finding anything out of the ordinary, so I'm hoping they'll do the same again here. And this time, we'll thoroughly investigate anything that catches their interest."

I nodded. It was a plausible plan, provided either of the dogs would become interested in anything. Just then, as if he was reading my thoughts, Sherlock tugged on his leash. Had he found something that quickly? Or was he simply anxious to begin exploring?

I took my jacket off and flung it over a tarp-covered chair just inside the living room on my left. I looked over at my girlfriend and passed her Watson's leash.

"I was about ready to say we should split up, but scratch that. I think I'd like us to stick together while we're in here. That way, we can both study the dogs and, hopefully, not miss anything."

Jillian flashed a smile at me and slid her arm through mine.

"It sounds like a plan. Watson? Are you ready to go? It looks like Sherlock wants to check out that door just behind us, to the right."

"There's not much through there, right?" I asked.

"I believe it's the den. Then, the room directly to the right of it is the billiard's room."

"There's more to see on this side," I said, as I tried to pull Sherlock toward the living room. "Come on, buddy, let's check out this side first, okay?"

Sherlock wouldn't budge an inch. I actually tried to pull him over to me, but the little corgi dropped as low as he could go to the ground and threw his weight in the opposite direction. The meaning was clear. He didn't want to go that way.

"Fine," I sighed. "Right, it is. Come on, gang, let's head to … okay, he doesn't want the den."

"Looks like he wants to go to the billiard's room," Jillian observed. "Come on, Watson. Let's follow Sherlock, okay?"

The small red and white corgi shook her collar, looked adoringly up at Jillian, and then myself, and then turned to watch her packmate trot toward the large double doors on the right. This room, I decided, as we all stepped through the doorway, must have been home to the snooker table currently sitting in the basement. Was Jillian planning on keeping this room as it was originally intended?

"What are you thinking about?" Jillian wanted to know. "You are either zoning or are in deep contemplation about something. Care to share?"

"Snooker."

Jillian blinked at me, "Huh?"

"I was just wondering if you were planning on keeping this room as a game room."

"Oh. As a matter of fact, I was."

"Perfect."

We stepped into the large, mostly empty room and

eyed the covered furniture that had been placed along the wall's perimeter. There were also several giant paintings on the walls, and when I say giant, I mean these suckers were huge. Several were almost floor to ceiling. One was a variant of the *Dogs Playing Poker* motif, while another reminded me of the ballerina on a tightrope picture found inside the Haunted Mansion in Disneyland. And the third?

I'll admit. This one was strange. It depicted a dark cavern, with fog—or mist, I guess—covering parts of the ground. And, I swear I could see what looked like a pair of eyes staring out from the depths of the cavern. What a picture like this was doing in here was beyond me.

"That's a little on the creepy side," I decided.

Jillian studied the painting and finally nodded. "Agreed. That, I'm sorry to say, will be one of the first things to go in this room."

Sherlock, much to my surprise, plunked his butt down in front of the creepy painting and stared up at it, unblinking. A few moments later, Watson joined him. I tried to give Sherlock's leash a gentle pull, indicating I wanted to leave, but Sherlock again decided he didn't want to move.

"Now what?" I asked, as I returned to the painting to give it a second glance. "It's dark and it's creepy, buddy. Let it go. There's much more pleasant things to see in here. Trust me, okay?"

Sherlock wasn't having it. He looked up at the huge picture, whined, and then looked back at me. I eyed Jillian before turning back to the painting. All right, Sherlock wanted a closer look?

"I'm not sure what you want me to see here," I admitted, as I ran my hands along the surface. "I ... hmm."

"What is it?" Jillian wanted to know, as she appeared

by my side.

I gently rapped my knuckles on the painting.

"Do you hear that?" I asked.

"It sounds like you're knocking on wood," Jillian decided.

I nodded. "Right. *Hollow* wood. Let me see something."

I gently gripped the picture's frame and pulled, intent on seeing what was on the other side. Imagine my surprise as I discovered the frame seemed to be a part of the wall itself. That picture wasn't going anywhere anytime soon. Confused, I knocked on a section of wall to the left of the painting.

"Sounds normal," I said. I moved to the other side of the painting and knocked again. "Same thing. It sounds like what you'd expect to hear if someone knocked on a wall. However, when I knock on the painting..."

I moved back to the picture and knocked again.

"It *does* sound hollow!" Jillian excitedly agreed.

"Coupled with the fact that the frame doesn't pull away from the wall suggests ... let's see."

I began poking and prodding the painting. Jillian, on the other hand, began running her hands along the frame. Once she hit the lower left corner, she let out an exclamation of surprise. I then heard a soft click and the entire painting—minus the frame—swung inward, like a door.

"Way to go, Sherlock!" I exclaimed, as I gave the corgi an enthusiastic scratching behind his ears. Not wanting Watson to feel left out, I did the same for her. "I'm liking this place more and more. What opened it? Was there something on the frame?"

"There's a small button," Jillian confirmed. "Should we

see where it goes?"

I pointed at the dark, narrow passageway.

"I think we're going to need flashlights if we're going to try and navigate through that."

Jillian held up her phone and waggled it.

"I've got my phone. So do you. That's two flashlights. Will that do?"

I activated the LED flash on my phone and held it high.

"Follow me, m'lady."

"After you, kind sir," Jillian returned, giggling.

We followed the narrow, dusty corridor for at least five minutes, stopping only to pick up the dogs a few times so they wouldn't have to jump over some fallen debris in the way. Before I knew it, the passageway had ended, and I was running my hands along the smooth surface of the wall directly in front of me.

"What do you have there?" Jillian wanted to know.

I raised my hand so I could illuminate as much of the area in front of me as possible.

"Well, we've got a wall, only it feels perfectly smooth. It's odd."

"Smooth, like tile?"

I ran my hands along the surface.

"I don't feel any grout lines, or any breaks in the tile. I'm going to have to say no, it's not tile."

"Marble?" Jillian suggested.

"That'd be one helluva piece of marble," I remarked, as I shone my light to the left and right of the dead-end hallway. "I ... hello. What's this?"

I stepped on a small lever I could see in the lower right corner of the wall. As before, with the painting, the entire wall swung open. Jillian and I took several steps backward so we could peer through the doorway to what lay beyond.

"I remember this room," Jillian said, as we emerged from the passageway. "This is that area we figured was the servant's dining room. I wonder why this room is connected to the billiard's room."

We took several steps out into the room and turned to see why we hadn't noticed this room had a secret entrance before. As it turns out, this room had wall-to-wall paneling. I remember thinking it was seriously outdated, but I have a feeling it was purposely used to disguise this door. The hidden door, when closed, practically disappeared into the paneling.

"Good job, Sherlock. Now that we're here, let's see if there's anything else to discover, okay?"

There wasn't. We spent nearly an hour in the northern half of the house. We searched the servants' rooms, the rear entrance to the house, and the pantry. We didn't get so much as a woof until we hit the kitchen.

"Awwooooo!" Sherlock howled.

Watson yipped excitedly.

"What's gotten them so riled up?" I wanted to know. I looked around the kitchen and shrugged. "Aside from needing a complete makeover, I don't see anything in here that stands out."

Jillian pointed at Sherlock.

"Let's see where he wants to go."

We were promptly led over to the wall opposite the stove. It had a small, semi-circular table on it, with three chairs. Sherlock ignored the furniture and gazed at the wall. The little corgi sat, unblinking, for so long that he inevitably snorted, looked up at me, and whined.

"Help me move these chairs, Zachary," Jillian said.

After we had cleared the wall of all the furniture, both Jillian and I began studying the surface. I didn't see any hidden buttons, or secret levers, or anything at all which would make this wall stand out. What had caught the dogs' attention?

At this time, I noticed Jillian was now running her hands along the surface, as though she believed the wall was hiding a door. However, I quickly shed my skeptical expression as her hand stopped at one specific point and she knocked. Intrigued, I stepped closer.

"What is it?"

"There's a depression right here," Jillian reported. "Let me show you. Here, put your hand next to mine. Do you feel that?"

"It's like there's a dip here," I decided. "And then was wallpapered over. How big is the area?"

"Not very. I'd say it's less than six square inches."

"Are you planning on keeping this wallpaper?"

"Heavens, no."

I unsheathed my multi-tool I kept on my belt and pulled out one of its blades.

"Would you mind?"

"Not at all."

I carefully cut around the area Jillian had discovered. Peeling the old wallpaper away, like I was removing a reluctant sticker from a newly purchased item, Jillian and I both let out twin grunts as we saw what lay beneath: a perfect circle, set inside a larger square. Directly in the middle of the circle was what looked like an aging label, which had lost its adhesive, and had begun pulling away from the surface. I removed the label and then whistled with amazement.

It was a keyhole.

"I don't suppose you have the key to this, do you?" I asked.

Jillian shrugged. "I didn't even know this was here. If I were to venture a guess, then I'd say no, I don't. But, let me check the key ring the realtor gave me."

Much to our surprise, we learned the key was included. Then again, the house key fit the lock, so it wasn't too surprising. Jillian wordlessly inserted the key and twisted to the right, and then when nothing happened, to the left.

We heard a loud click.

A large section of the wall suddenly shifted, which resulted in the tearing of wallpaper. I ran my hands along the surface, pressing in here and there. Satisfied I had deduced what happened, I turned to her.

"A door just opened," I reported, "but because of the wallpaper, it can't open."

Jillian slowly looked around the room and then snapped her fingers.

"Of course! Do you remember the picture Katherine showed us? The one of the kitchen and the cases of booze? That was taken in this kitchen, I'm sure of it!"

"The stove is in the wrong spot," I recalled. "Are you sure?"

"They evidently moved the stove, but yes, this is the same kitchen. I think we just found the compartment where the Highland family hid their booze."

I retrieved my knife and held it up.

"Shall I?"

Jillian nodded. "Please do."

I ran my knife along the distended wall, applying

enough pressure to cut through the wallpaper. Acting like I was opening the world's biggest box, I made several slices along the paper, freeing the door. It immediately swung open. Sure enough, we saw a room that couldn't have been more than five feet deep, but it had to have extended the entire length of the wall, since it had to be at least twenty feet long.

"What are those?" Jillian wanted to know.

She was pointing at something that was leaning up against the wall, and like just about all the other furnishings in this house, it was covered by a tarp. I pulled the tarp away to reveal a couple of paintings. One was a picture of what looked like New Orleans, which I have to say that I liked. And the other?

"It's the Monet!" Jillian breathed.

"The same one from Katherine's photo album?"

Jillian nodded excitedly, "Yes! The very same! Zachary, if this is a legitimate Monet, then it'll be worth millions."

"If it's a legitimate Monet," I began, "then that means it was stolen. We should track down who it belongs to and give it back."

Jillian rose up on her tiptoes and gave me a quick peck on my cheek.

"And that's why I love you, Zachary. You're always trying to do the right thing."

The house fell deathly quiet. I cleared my throat.

"Er, what was that?"

Jillian froze as she realized what she had said.

"Umm…"

"You love me?" I repeated, as I turned to look at her.

"Oh, that just slipped right out, didn't it? I'm sorry. You probably aren't ready to hear that, are you?"

I took her hand in mine, brought it up to my lips, and planted a kiss on her fingers.

"I thought for certain I was going to freak out just then, but right now, I can't stop smiling."

A look of relief washed over Jillian's face.

"I love you, too, Jillian. And, let me add, I didn't think I'd ever be able to say those words to anyone again."

Jillian threw her arms around me and hugged me tight. Both corgis craned their necks to look up at us as they watched us embrace. After a few moments had passed, Sherlock evidently decided a corgi intervention was necessary and woofed to get our attention.

"Don't worry, pretty boy," Jillian told the corgi, as she squatted down to put her arms around the dog. "I would never hurt your daddy."

Watson whined and then wiggled her way under Jillian's arm.

"That goes for you, too, little girl."

I passed Sherlock's leash to Jillian.

"What are you doing?" she wanted to know.

"I want to see if there's anything else in there besides paintings."

There wasn't. Holding my phone up high, I walked up and down that narrow hidden storage chamber several times. Those two pictures were the only things stored in the concealed room. Shrugging, I emerged from the hidden room, closed the door, and reclaimed Sherlock's leash. I gave him a good scratching behind his ears.

"You are proving you're worth your weight in gold, pal. Keep it up, okay?" I turned to Jillian. "Now what?"

Jillian pointed back toward the foyer.

"I say we go back there. Now that we've discovered

this secret passage, let's see if there's anything else that attracts the dogs' attention."

Nodding, I gave a gentle tug on the leash to get Sherlock's attention. Back in the foyer, I had just taken a few steps toward the billiard's room when my arm was yanked backwards. Surprised, I looked back at Sherlock. The little corgi was looking pointedly at the door leading into the den.

"What, you want to go in there now? Sure, why not."

I pushed the door open and allowed Sherlock to enter first. The inquisitive little corgi trotted over to a tarp-covered desk, sniffed the base of it, and then moved off. Bemused, I followed the little dog as we walked around the perimeter of the small room. Glancing around, I could see that several of the walls had built-in bookcases. Those that didn't had large paintings on them. Detecting movement in my peripheral vision, I looked to my right and watched Watson and Jillian walk in the opposite direction. I figured in twenty seconds, we were going to meet in the middle.

Wrong again.

Watson stopped after only a few steps. She lifted her head, sniffed at the corner of another large painting, and then turned to look up at Jillian.

"What have you found, pretty girl?" Jillian asked. I watched her hesitantly try to pull the painting away from the wall. It didn't budge. She tapped the painting itself, but after a few moments, she gave up. "Well, there's no secret door behind this one. It feels like there's nothing back there but solid stone."

I pointed at the picture.

"What's it a picture of? Maybe it's relevant."

Jillian took a few steps back to better study the picture.

"Well, I'm not sure. It's just a picture of a thatched cottage in the middle of the woods. There's a girl out front, and she appears to be sitting at a loom."

"A loom?" I repeated.

"It's a weaving machine," Jillian translated.

"Gotcha. All right, I'm not sure why this caught Watson's attention, but ... hey, let's do this." I pulled out my cell and snapped a picture. "We can study it later. Then ... Sherlock? Watson? Where are you two off to now?"

The corgis led us from the den, over to the north lobby, and through a door on the right. I looked up at the 2nd floor, seeing how the dogs had led us to the base of the smaller second staircase. However, Sherlock pulled us to a closed door instead.

"And what do we have through here? It's ... a bathroom. That's cute, guys. I know you don't have to go potty. You two both went just before we got here. So, what's so important about this bathroom?"

"Did you find something in there?" Jillian asked, from somewhere behind me.

"It's a bathroom, and no, I don't see anything in here. It's small, so there's not a lot of places to stash anything. Fine, I'll take a pic, Sherlock. Stop looking at me like that."

Picture taken, the dogs led us back to the stairs, and up. I silently groaned to myself as I realized that a thorough search of this floor would take a long while. I remembered there were at least six bedrooms up there, and that included a huge master suite. It was going to be dark out before we were done searching this floor.

As I have mentioned numerous times, I'm wrong quite often.

We were promptly led to the large bedroom in the

southeastern corner of the house. Consequently, it was located directly over the billiard's room. Stepping inside, I had barely time to turn on the lights before both dogs pulled us over to the closet.

"I swear, there had better not be a mouse in there," I grumbled softly to myself.

I glared at Sherlock, who gazed up at me with an innocent expression on his face. The corgis watched me closely as I stretched out a hand to open the door. What we found was … an empty closet.

"Swell, guys. There's nothing here. Would you care to…?"

I trailed off as both dogs entered the closet and sniffed along the left-hand wall.

"There's no place to hang clothes on this side," Jillian observed. "See? There's a metal pole stretching across the right side. But the left? Nothing."

"That really doesn't mean anything. Maybe they had to store some boxes. You'd be able to stack them quite high in here."

Both dogs continued to sniff along the ground. Curious, I squatted down and gave the dogs a pat.

"What's up, guys? Do you smell something on the ground?"

"There are light scuff marks," Jillian said, after she knelt down beside me. "Zachary, I think this wall moves, too."

"Let's find out, shall we?"

Rising to my feet, I started to push and prod at the wall, fully expecting it to move. Nothing. The wall felt— and looked—as immobile as you'd expect a wall to be in a closet. Undeterred, I increased pressure, to the point I was leaning my full weight onto the wall. And, unsurprisingly, that accomplished jack squat.

Watson came to the rescue. The timid red and white corgi, who had up to this time been sitting motionless next to Sherlock, suddenly rose to her feet, gave herself a solid shake, and then moved to the opposite wall of the closet and sat. I should also point out that this particular closet was tiled and she had chosen the tile closest to the door on the right.

We all heard a *click*, and lo and behold, the wall swung inward. As one, Jillian and I looked over at Watson, who seemingly had a smile on her face as she panted. Sherlock snorted, as if to say *beginner's luck*, and eagerly pushed forward, intent on investigating. With our flashlights held high, we entered yet another secret compartment.

I sighed as I looked around. This one didn't contain any jewelry, either. There were no paintings, but there was a single open box against the far corner of the space, covered by a crumbling newspaper.

"Well, let's see what we've got," I said, as I slid the box close. "We have one newspaper, and it is dated from the early 1960s. We have something that kinda looks like … like … wow. I have no idea what this is."

Jillian leaned over to look into the box.

"Well, I see a … this? Really, Zachary? You know full well what that is."

As though I was reaching for a golden idol, and pretending that the room we were in would suddenly collapse in on itself if I touched it, I lifted the rotary telephone from the box and held it up to the light.

"I am so amazed. I have never seen one of these in such pristine condition before."

"You silly man," Jillian giggled. "What else is in there?"

"Well, we have the phone and we have what looks like, um…" I trailed off as I felt my face flame up. What in the world could it be? "You tell me."

I pulled the strange contraption out of the box and held it up. It looked like an elongated newel post, only it had been cut in half and mounted on a flat base. Also present was a handle, which presumably the user could spin in order to narrow or widen the strange wooden object.

My poor mind kept falling into the gutter, and try as I might, I couldn't begin to imagine what the device could be. Thankfully, Jillian was much smarter than me. She provided the answer.

"It's an antique hat press. You place your hat here, and then turn the handle there. It reshapes your hat, as needed."

"And you know this *how*?" I curiously asked.

"My grandmother had one of these. It looked remarkably like this one, making this French, I believe. Is there anything else?"

"Well, nothing you need to know about."

"What does that mean?" Jillian cautiously asked. "Would you tell me, please?"

I shrugged. "Don't say I didn't warn you. Very well. We have not one, or two, but three dead bugs in here. From the look of it, I'd say they were…"

"No!" Jillian all but shouted. "You're right. I don't need to know. I was already planning on having this place fumigated once the work was done."

"Well, I think we should … hey, hang on. Jillian? You're not going to believe this."

She poked her head into the closet.

"What is it?"

I pointed at the back of the secret room, which was

nearly ten feet behind me.

"This isn't the back," I reported, as I strode away from the door. "This closet makes another sharp turn, just like the one in the master bedroom. There's … whoa! Wow, that was close."

"What's the matter?" Jillian called, from behind me. "Zachary, are you okay?"

"Yeah, I'm okay. I didn't see this here. Jillian, there is a staircase here! It's one of those tight, spiral ones that's barely wide enough to admit a person."

"I'm coming. I want to see this."

Jillian appeared at my side, as did both corgis. Sherlock lowered his nose and sniffed along the ground. Within moments, the little corgi had snorted several times, seeing how there was a thick layer of dust on the ground.

"Let's see where this goes!" Jillian said, as she hurried by me, handing me Watson's leash as she did.

We cautiously made our way down the stairs. I heard Jillian announce we had hit the bottom, and just like that, light was suddenly streaming in. I emerged into the bright light and looked around. We were back in the den! I turned to look back at the darkened passage we had just come through. Sure enough, the doorway was another painting, and it was the one with the thatched cottage and the girl working at the loom. This time, the door had swung outward, into the room, and from the looks of it, the door itself had a layer of stone mortared on its surface. That was why Jillian had believed there wasn't a passageway behind it. Watson had known, of course. I can only presume she must have smelled something behind the painting.

"Have I mentioned that I'm really enjoying this house?" I asked.

Jillian laughed. "Once or twice. Let me guess. You'd

prefer it if I left all these secret passageways alone."

"Oh, heck yeah!" I agreed. "You can have a field day with that. Think how that would read on a flyer! *Pomme Valley's newest bed and breakfast, serving up the experience of a lifetime! Find the hidden passages and win a prize!*"

Jillian laughed again as she looked around the den.

"Aunt Hilda sure didn't like putting all her eggs in one basket, did she?"

I nodded. "I hadn't thought of it that way. I guess if the house was ever raided, and some of these rooms were discovered, then it'd be highly unlikely that *all* secret rooms would be discovered, so she'd still be in business."

"Precisely. She must have ... Zachary? What's Sherlock looking at now?"

I found Sherlock sniffing along one of the three bookcases recessed into the walls. All the shelves were empty, of course, but that didn't stop the tri-colored corgi from giving one of the cases a second look. He sniffed the base of the bookcase a few times and then promptly sat.

I stepped up to the bookcase and handed Sherlock's leash to Jillian. I gently prodded and pulled at various shelves until there was yet another soft *click* and the entire bookcase swung out of the wall, into the room. I squatted low so I could peer into the dark recesses of yet another secret storage compartment. This one, I noted, with growing excitement, wasn't empty. There were crates— which contained whiskey—and covered paintings on the left side, and the right had more open crates. I could see various items poking up and out of their respective boxes.

"More antiques," I guessed. "Think any of her jewelry will be in there?"

Jillian shook her head. "I doubt it. Look at the number

of secrets we've uncovered in this house, and it's all thanks to the dogs. Can you even imagine how many more spots like this must exist in this house? Hilda certainly knew how to keep prying eyes away from her things."

"It's getting late," I said, as I noticed the time on my watch. "We should probably get going. Can I buy you dinner?"

"Who am I to turn down dinner from a handsome man?" Jillian said, as she batted her eyes at me.

"Come on, guys," I said, as I took both leashes in my hand. "That's enough exploring for one day. We're outta here."

Sherlock, on the other hand, had different plans. He pulled me, Clydesdale-style, back to the bathroom off the north lobby.

"What are we doing back here? There's nothing to check here, unless you think there's a secret door under the sink."

Jillian chuckled, "Based on what we found earlier, you never know."

I sighed, looked down at Sherlock, and groaned.

"Fine. I'll check, okay?"

As I expected, there wasn't anything there. I checked the sinks (there were two), checked the cabinets, and even felt along all the walls. I checked the toilet, which was located through a door on the other side of the bathroom, and felt along the tile. I should also point out that Sherlock kept his attention focused on the sink. Exasperated, I finally pulled out my cell and snapped a few pics, just for my own piece of mind. Thankfully, that seemed to mollify the little corgi.

"Are we good now, your Royal Canineship? Let's go home."

Once again, I couldn't help but feel we were missing something. Every other thing the dogs had focused on in this house turned up something. However, this bathroom? It was the only strike. There *had* to be something I was missing. As I learned later, what I missed had the potential of busting this case wide open. For once, though, I'm proud to say that I caught my mistake fairly quickly, as you'll soon see.

SEVEN

Come on, you sucker," I growled, as I gripped the controls tightly in my hands. I yanked back on the control stick and hissed with frustration as I felt the resistance on the arm. "Why won't you *move*? Get off my land, you miserable, ugly-looking son of a..."

Sherlock's growl cut me off, mid-sentence. It seemed to be a new favorite pastime of his: interrupting me in mid-rant. Seriously, Jillian must have trained him to do that.

Yeah, I know what you're thinking. Context is required in order to understand what is going on. Well, it was now Tuesday of the following week. The work had resumed on Highland House, with Robert the foreman assuring us that there'd be no more mishaps or delays. Thus far, he had been right. There certainly hadn't been any more fatalities.

Yes, it was still early in the week, but perhaps the ghost had finally moved on?

I was currently sitting in my all-time favorite toy, my John Deere tractor. Even though nothing had been finalized, and no plans had been officially drawn up, I was already clearing the land next to the winery in preparation for the new warehouse. I knew this was the day to get things underway when, after wandering outside first thing in the morning, I noticed there weren't any cars parked along the side of the winery. That meant Caden wasn't conducting a class at the winery today. No class meant no students, which meant I was finally able to get at that god-forsaken stump sitting directly in the middle of the impromptu parking lot. The stump even had one short branch left on it, down near the base, which looked remarkably like a middle finger. Every time I looked at it, I swear it was flipping me off.

Not any more, pal. Today's the day when I flip you the bird back. So, with the dogs sitting next to me on the small buddy seat on my left, and me at the controls of my big toy with its front loader attachment, we began our battle. The SfH (Stump from Hell) came out swinging, as clearly this thing had what felt like roots that were extending several miles beneath the surface. My tractor was strong, but even it struggled to pull SfH out of the ground.

"Let's try this," I said aloud, as I repositioned the tractor on the other side of the stump. "Let's clear away some dirt here, like this ... good. Now, if we push the bucket underneath that root there, and ... nope. Damn. There's just nothing for the bucket to latch on to. Maybe ... wait a minute. Of course! Why didn't I think about that before? You two stay right here."

I grabbed my gloves and hopped outside. Turning, I reached back inside the cab, under the buddy seat, to grab the chain I had forgotten was there. The only drawback was, with both hands preoccupied, and my face mere inches from the buddy seat, it put me within striking range of both dogs' tongues. Yep. I got doggie kisses.

"Ack! Pbttth! What are you doing? Stop it! Blech!"

Both corgis seemed to delight in my misery. The dogs knew that both of my hands were full, so they took full advantage of the situation. I swear each of them took turns, first one lick by Watson, then one by Sherlock. Annnd… repeat.

"Okay, you goobers. That's enough. Thank you. My face is clean. Now, stay there. We're going to win this battle yet."

With the chain securely wrapped around the stump, and hooked to the tractor's bucket, I slowly pulled back on the lifting lever. The tractor groaned, and I had to rev the engine to make certain I didn't stall it, but I was finally rewarded with several loud cracks and snaps. SfH then lurched sideways, as though I delivered a fatal blow.

"I've got you now, you bastard," I grumbled, as I adjusted the tractor's position. I looked at the dogs and grinned. "This will be one less thing I'll be charged for when we do break ground on the new warehouse. The more I can do, the less I have to pay."

Sherlock gazed at me and blinked a few times. Then he turned to watch as the stump finally, *finally* lifted free.

"Hey, you got it!" I heard a voice exclaim.

I looked over at the winery. Caden was standing there, watching the proceedings.

"I swear I'm gonna grind this thing up and use it for

mulch," I vowed, as I gave my winemaster a grin.

Caden laughed and disappeared back inside the winery. Just then, my cell rang. It was Jillian. Oh, man, I hope she wasn't calling to let me know there was another problem at Highland House.

"Hi, Jillian. Is everything okay?"

"Yes. No problems that I'm aware of."

"Good. What can I do for you?"

"Did you take pictures of all the antiques we found when we were searching the house this last weekend?"

I thought about it for a few moments.

"I have some, but not all. Whenever the dogs expressed interest in something, I took a picture. So, I do know I have a couple. What did you need?"

"I was talking to Burt, over at his shop, and he's expressed interest in anything I don't want to keep at the house. Plus, I wanted to see if he could identify a few things I couldn't."

Burt Johnson was the owner of Hidden Relic Antiques, the local antique shop in town. At well over 6'8", he had to be the most fearsome, intimidating person living in PV. Thankfully, I can say that his looks are deceiving. He's quite nice, very friendly, and is a fan of the dogs.

"Makes sense. Let me check my phone."

"Do you need to call me back?"

"No, I'm good. This tractor came equipped with a Bluetooth stereo. That way I can talk and still work at the same time. At the moment, I can search through the phone without hanging up on you. I think."

I heard Jillian giggle. Pulling up the photo album on my phone, I started going through my recent pictures. There were a few in there that I'm sure Burt would want to see.

"Yeah, I have a couple. Would you like me to send them to you?"

"Would you? That'd be great! Thank you, Zachary."

"You're welcome. I can ..."

I trailed off as the picture of the bathroom and its dual sinks appeared on my phone. Something had caught my eye, and it was something that made it feel as though time itself had just skidded to a stop. There, clearly visible in the sink, was a tiny blob of bright green goo. What was it? Well, I knew without a doubt what it was: toothpaste.

Did you get that? There was toothpaste in the sink! That clearly meant someone had brushed their teeth in there. No wonder Sherlock kept trying to bring it to my attention. The million dollar question was, who had brushed their teeth in that sink? Could it have been one of the workers? Or, more disturbingly, could it have been our ghost??

"Jillian? Are you still there?"

"Of course I'm still here. What is it? You sound as though you just saw a ghost."

"Funny you should say that. Where are you right now?"

"At Highland House. Why?"

"Is Robert there, too?"

"I saw him earlier. I think he's outside, overseeing some roof work. Why? You're starting to concern me."

"Listen to me. This is very important. I need you to go find Robert, as quick as you can. Get somewhere private and put this call on speaker, okay?"

"Very well. I'm walking outside now. Hmm, I don't see ... there he is. Robert! Could you come here a second? I'm sorry, I know this sounds strange, but I need you to come with me. Zachary is on the line and he needs to ask you something. Plus, we need to do it in private. Hang on, Zachary. We're going to go to my car. I sure do hope this is nothing bad."

"I think this might answer a lot of questions, but before I say anything, I need to talk to Robert first. I need to know about his crew."

"The workers? Well, we're both here now, Zachary. Now, can you please tell me what's going on?"

"Robert, are you there?"

"I'm here, Mr. Anderson. What can I do for you?"

"I know this is going to sound crazy, but I need to ask you something: have you ever seen any of your workers brush their teeth in the house? More specifically, in the bathroom on the northern side of the house?"

"¿Que es esto? Brush their teeth? At a job site? No, Mr. Anderson. Trust me, no one has used any of the facilities here. It's a zero-tolerance rule I have. Why?"

"What about any further incidents?" I pressed. "Have you, or any of your workers, noticed anything strange?"

"Nothing that could possibly be related to this," Robert assured me. "Please, Mr. Anderson, tell me what has gotten you so riled up. What's happened?"

"I have a picture here of the bathroom," I slowly explained. "Jillian asked me to look for pictures of antiques, but before I could find those, I found this picture. In the sink is clearly a dollop of toothpaste. If none of your laborers used that bathroom, then…"

I heard Jillian gasp with alarm. Robert, on the other hand, did exactly what I expected him to do. He cursed. Quite well, actually. Thankfully, it was in Spanish.

"I don't like this," I heard Jillian say.

"I don't, either. Robert, you suggested something has

happened there?"

"You did?" Jillian's voice asked.

"I'm sure it's just a case of someone being forgetful," the foreman explained.

"Do go on," I heard Jillian's voice say. "What did you mean by that? Someone has been 'forgetful'?"

I suddenly thought back to the missing scaffolding pins and grunted irritably.

"You're missing things, aren't you?"

"*Si, señor.* Several tools have been reported missing. I just assumed they were either left behind, at home, or else perhaps someone picked up a tool that didn't belong to them. Are you suggesting they were stolen?"

"I am, yes."

"It cannot be any of the crew," Robert insisted. "I personally vetted each of them myself. It has to be an outsider. Now, I will say that several workers from the first crew did return for work, but I still don't think it could be any of them."

"Then that would suggest someone has been inside my house!" Jillian protested. "Robert, I need those locks changed out. Today."

"Do not worry, señora. I will take care of it myself."

"I prefer señorita, if you don't mind," Jillian's voice wryly said.

"Ah! *¿Habla Español, señorita?*"

"*Un poquito. Tuve cuatro años en la escuela secondaria. Hablo un poco, pero puedo entender más.*"

Jillian spoke Spanish? And based on the Great Frog Leg Debacle that happened last year, I knew she also spoke French. Wow. Is there anything this lady couldn't do?

"Umm, guys? For those of us who don't speak Spanish,

could someone clue me in to what's going on?"

"*Tu amor es algo especial, amigo.*"

"Huh?" I stammered.

"My apologies, Mr. Anderson. I was giving Ms. Cooper a compliment. She speaks Spanish very well. I am impressed."

"And that makes two of us," I admitted. "You learn something new every day."

"Oh, don't make a big deal of it," Jillian told me. "I'm not fluent. I can get by, that's it. If you want a cold beer, or need to know where the bathroom is, then I'm your girl."

Robert laughed, and I ended up chuckling.

"Jillian? Would you do me a favor?"

"Of course, Zachary. What do you need?"

"I need you to either get out of the house, at least until I can get there, or please have someone with you at all times."

"There's no such thing as ghosts," Jillian reminded me.

"I know there isn't. I'm thinking more along the lines of a he-who-is-responsible-for-this-ghost-might-still-be-in-the-house type of spook."

"And who do we think is responsible?" Jillian asked.

"That, unfortunately, I cannot tell you."

"Mr. Anderson, don't you worry about Ms. Cooper," Robert's voice cut in. "I have plenty to do inside the house. I will personally keep an eye on her for you."

"Thank you, Robert. That means a lot. Jillian? I'll get over there just as soon as I'm no longer needed at the winery."

"I'm sure I'll be fine, Zachary. But thank you. I look forward to seeing you soon."

A few hours later, I was—once again—standing inside

Highland House. Jillian and Robert were there, in the kitchen, going over plans on what needed to be changed. Jillian was pointing here and there, and Robert offered comments to whatever Jillian was saying. Leaving them to their discussion, I headed straight for the north lobby. Would I really find toothpaste in the sink?

As it turns out, the answer was a definitive *no*. I stood two feet in front of the aforementioned sink and stared at the meticulously clean bowl. Frowning, I pulled out my cell and compared the picture to the real thing. One thing was abundantly clear: someone had cleaned up their mess. The question was, who?

"What did you find, Zachary?" Jillian asked, as she stepped up beside me.

I pointed at the clean sink.

"Absolutely nothing. See?"

"Oh, good. So, there's nothing I need to worry about?"

I showed her the picture I had taken the last time we were here together. A reverse pinch on the screen zoomed in on the bathroom sink. I then pointed at the gelatinous substance clearly visible in the photo.

"What do you think that is?"

"Why, it's toothpaste!" Jillian exclaimed. She turned to look for Robert, who was standing nearby, working on some electrical wiring. "Robert? Would you come over here, please?"

Robert nodded. "Of course. The electrical short I was telling you about wasn't located at that socket. Sí, it's old, but it's still serviceable. What's this? A picture of the bathroom?"

"It's the one I told you about, taken the last time the two of us were here, together," Jillian explained.

"Do you see that right there?" I asked, as I held the phone out to Robert. "Doesn't that look like toothpaste?"

"It most certainly does," Robert agreed, growing angry. "I know my guys are not responsible for this. However, just to be completely certain, I will go double check."

I noticed Jillian was slowly looking around the room, as if she expected someone to come popping out of the walls at any time. I was about ready to suggest that it was, more than likely, one of the workers had simply spit something in one of the sinks as they went by, but now refused to come forward for fear of reprisal, when Sherlock woofed. Surprised, I looked down at the inquisitive corgi, only he wasn't looking at me. Both he and Watson were looking behind us, directly at the living room.

"All right, you two. It serves me right for not paying attention earlier. Sherlock? You've found something? Lead the way, pal."

Sherlock pulled me back to the living room and headed straight for the drop cloth covered sofa. Staring at the large piece of furniture with bewilderment, I could only wonder what had attracted the dog's attention *this* time. The one thing I did know was that he hadn't given the couch a second look the last couple of times we had been in here.

"What's with him?" Jillian wondered aloud.

"I don't know. There's something up with the couch. What do you think it means?"

"Feel free to take the tarp off, in case there's something underneath it."

Handing the leashes to Jillian, I pulled the tarp off the furniture, revealing a rectangular sofa with the arms and back of the same height. It was clean-lined, had solid wood legs and a tufted back. Plus, it was a deep red color, almost to the point of it being maroon.

"I really love this sofa," Jillian announced. "Only, I don't think the color will match anything I want to do in here. So, it'll be reupholstered. Do you like it? I found out it's classified as a *tuxedo* sofa."

"I like it," I decided. "It looks comfortable. Were you the one who covered it up in the first place?"

"No. Robert and his crew covered everything."

"Hmm. Did you see the couch before it was covered?"

"Yes. Why?"

I pointed at the sofa.

"Do you see anything different about it? I'm just trying to figure out why Sherlock was interested in it."

Jillian was silent as she studied the couch. After a few moments, she shook her head.

"I'm sorry. It looks the same to me."

"Well," I said, as I scratched my head. "we can…"

I trailed off as I watched Sherlock jam his snout under the couch and let out another woof. Watson mimicked him, only she let out a piteous whine, instead. Grumbling like I typically did whenever I had to retrieve a ball, or a dog toy, from underneath my own couch, I dropped down to my knees and gingerly lowered my head to peer under the couch.

Well, it wasn't a ball. However, it wasn't something that I wanted to find, either. And no, before you ask, it wasn't a body part. It was a clump of dirt. *Fresh* dirt.

Holding the clod of dirt in my hand, I rose to my feet and showed it to Jillian. Her eyes widened as she stared at the dirt.

"This hasn't been in here that long," I told her.

"If that's true, Zachary, then that confirms…"

"…someone has been in here besides us," I finished for her.

Jillian fished her cell out of her purse.

"I'm calling Vance. I don't like this at all."

In the process of doing the exact same thing, I put mine away and let Jillian make the call.

"Vance? It's Jillian. Can you please come over to Highland House? Someone has been in here, and I'm not sure if they're still in here somewhere, hiding. I don't feel safe in my own … what's that? Where's Zachary? He's right here. He was about to call you first, but I beat him to it."

Swell. She saw me cancel my call? That woman has the eyes of a hawk.

"Thank you, Vance. We'll be here waiting for you."

"He called me a sissy, didn't he?" I groaned.

"Not at all. I think he could tell from my voice that I was serious. He's on his way over here right now."

"We're not pulling him away from anything, are we?" I wanted to know.

"Actually, I think he was grateful for stepping away from his desk. Honestly? I think he sounded bored."

I shrugged. "Well, I'm happy we're here to, what, give him something to do? No, that didn't sound right."

Jillian smiled and patted my hand.

"I know what you meant."

Fifteen minutes later, Vance strode into the house. He caught sight of the dogs and immediately reached into his jacket pocket. Squatting down to their level, the detective gave the dogs their customary doggie biscuits. He looked up at the two of us and grinned.

"Hey, Zack. Jillian. Er, how are things with you two?"

Suddenly feeling silly for calling my detective friend

over for finding a clump of dirt, I held my arms behind my back.

"Good, buddy. Thanks. Listen, maybe we jumped the gun here."

"Except, we didn't," Jillian argued. "Zachary, show him the dirt."

"Dirt?" Vance skeptically asked. He took the sample I held out to him and studied it. "Where did you find this, again?"

I pointed at the couch.

"Under there."

"It's too recent to have been there long."

"Show him the picture of the toothpaste," Jillian urged.

Nodding, I pulled out my cell and brought up the photo of the bathroom sink and the drop of toothpaste clearly visible in it.

"I took this Sunday," I explained. "I didn't notice the toothpaste until today. When I came to check, the sink had been cleaned."

"Aren't there a number of guys who are constantly coming in and out of this place?"

"My guys didn't do this," Robert announced, as he appeared in the doorway. "The entire crew knows the house is off limits."

"And the dirt?" Vance pressed.

"While possible," Robert reluctantly admitted, "it's highly unlikely it came from one of us."

"You can't be sure of that," Vance insisted.

Robert pointed at his feet. For the first time, I noticed the foreman was wearing disposable polypropylene shoe covers over his boots.

"There's a box of these things just outside the door,"

he explained. "No one comes in here without a set of these on their shoes."

"I never noticed the plastic booties," Jillian admitted, as she watched one of the workers walk by. He, too, was wearing a set of the shoe covers.

"That makes two of us," I added. "So, do you believe us now? Dude, I'm telling you, someone was here, and it wasn't us."

"What do you want me to do? Search the house?"

I nodded. "I think that's a great start. I ... now what?"

The dogs, upon hearing my suggestion to begin a thorough search of the house, had jumped to their feet. They pulled on their leashes, anxious to be underway. I looked at Jillian and then over at Robert.

"She'll be fine, Mr. Anderson," Robert assured me. "Do your search. If you need anything, just holler."

"And if I start screaming?" I asked, with a grin on my face.

Robert stuck his hands in his pockets, looked over at Jillian, and returned the grin.

"If we hear any screaming, well, then I do suggest you keep up, señor."

I laughed and then gave the dogs some slack with their leashes. The first thing they did was pull me toward the servants' area, and the stairs leading down to the basement. Shrugging, I figured it'd be the best place to start searching, only how the dogs knew that, I didn't know. I gave up a long time ago when it came to trying to figure out how the dogs knew where to look for clues. Checking behind me to verify the guy with the gun was following, we headed down the steps.

"You're not really buying this malarkey with the

ghosts, are you?" Vance skeptically asked, as we arrived at the bottom of the stairs.

I slapped a hand on the wall and waited for the lights to kick on before I proceeded.

"Of course not."

"This coming from someone who believes mummies exist?"

"They *do* exist," I pointed out.

"Sorry. Let me rephrase that. You believe mummies can come to life and jump out at you from the shadows. Is that better?"

"Bite me. I never said that."

"Do I need to remind you about the mummy you believed was terrorizing the town several years ago?"

"Do I need to pull up the video from YouTube which shows you dancing in a Peter Pan outfit?" I countered.

Both references referred to a case involving a priceless Egyptian pendant, and it had been stolen by what I had originally thought of as a mummy. Vance had then vowed to take dancing lessons should Sherlock ever manage to locate it.

Let's just say that the *Dancing Detective* video has gone viral three times, and currently has over three million views. Anytime Vance tried to give me a hard time, I only had to reference that video, and usually he would be anxious to change the subject. And that's exactly what happened here.

"What do you think the dogs are after?" Vance asked, as we emerged into the basement.

I felt dual tugs on the leashes and let the dogs lead me over to a row of antique-looking wardrobes.

"I'm guessing there's something in one of these?" I theorized.

Much to my astonishment, I saw Vance reach back to rest his hand on his right hip, which I knew was where he kept his gun. He clearly wasn't taking any chances. We then watched as both dogs walked straight to one wardrobe in particular, settled themselves down (in unison), and then looked back at us.

"All right, I'll bite," Vance admitted. "Zack? Get them away from that thing. I'm gonna find out what's inside it."

With his right hand resting on his gun, Vance gingerly gripped the handle of one of the doors and then yanked it backwards, as though he expected a wall of junk to cascade out. As luck would have it, nothing was inside that wanted out. As a matter of fact, there wasn't anything inside the wardrobe at all.

"Well, that's a bust," I declared, as I gathered up the leashes and started to pull the dogs away. "Sherlock, you're losing your touch, pal."

"No, he's not," Vance argued.

I turned to see Vance peering closely at the bottom of the wardrobe.

"What is it?" I cautiously asked. "It's empty, right?"

"Right now, sure," Vance said, nodding. "but do you see this? Something was here, and it was dirty."

"Dirty?" I repeated, curious. "By any chance, does it match the clump of…?"

"It does," Vance interrupted. "Same consistency, same color."

The detective knocked a few times on the back of the wardrobe. Grunting with surprise, he placed both hands on the surface and shoved. There was a loud crunch, and suddenly, I could smell dank, musty air.

"Well, would you look at that?"

I leaned around Vance's body and noticed the dark, gaping hole that was once the back of the wardrobe. It had a secret door! How cool! No, wait. Wrong emotion. That meant there *was* someone hiding in the house. With my girlfriend.

"Oh, no," I muttered.

Vance pulled his weapon free of its holster.

"My sentiments exactly. Stay behind me. I don't suppose you have a flashlight on you, do you?"

I held up my phone and turned on the LED.

"Kinda. Would this do?"

"It will for now, thanks. Come on. Let's see where this goes."

I followed Vance down a steep tunnel. Reaching out to let my hand run along the surface of the tunnel, I could feel hard-packed earth. Someone had dug this tunnel, and I was pretty sure, judging from the smoothness of the floor and the walls, this tunnel has been here for quite some time. Perhaps Dame Highland used it as another hiding place for her numerous business dealings?

Vance held a finger to his lips. Both dogs, who had been noisily panting, surprising fell silent. I narrowed my eyes. Why was it the dogs always seemed to pay closer attention to someone *besides* you? I'm 99.99 percent certain that, if I had been holding the gun and had held a finger to my lips, I would have been thoroughly ignored.

Vance then pointed down at the ground. There, running along the far right side of the tunnel, was a black cord. I could see that it was a heavy-duty extension cord. How was it we didn't see this sticking out of the wardrobe back in the basement?

The four of us silently emerged into a large, crude

room. A quick glance around the area confirmed we had, indeed, located the lair for our notorious ghost. Over on a pallet in the far corner lay an assortment of power tools. Robert's missing tools?

I felt a tap on my shoulder. Vance was pointing at a sack full of something near the pallet. I squatted low and saw the bag was full of pins. Then my eyes widened. Were these the missing scaffolding pins, which resulted in a man's death?

"There's no one here," Vance decided, nearly five minutes later. "This room isn't that big, but you can clearly see this is where our perp has been living."

"Living? Down here? You're kidding."

"No, I'm serious. Check it out. There's a hot plate over there. That's where the extension cord ends. And over there? A cheap mattress. Hang on, I think I see a light."

A few moments later, bright light flooded the small area, affording us with the ability to see all four corners of what I was now calling the second basement.

I felt a tug on one of the leashes. Looking down, I expected to find Sherlock, who was trying to attract my attention. Not this time. It was Watson, and she was looking straight at a white plastic bag, like a grocery bag.

"Whatcha got?" Vance inquired, once he saw me peering into the bag.

"Soup, beans, and an assortment of canned goods. You're right. This guy has been here a while."

Sherlock sniffed the air a few times and then turned his head to look at the hot plate. Curious, Vance and I squatted next to the small electrical appliance and felt around the stump it was sitting on. Vance suddenly cursed under his breath as he reached behind the stump and came back with an open can of soup.

It was still warm.

"Vance, I think we spooked him," I nervously said, as I peered suspiciously around the hidden basement. "Do you think he's still here?"

In response, both corgis suddenly perked up and they barked. Loudly. Then, in unison, they bolted for the tunnel which led back up to the real basement. Anticipating what they were going to do, Vance and I were already heading in the same direction.

That's when we heard it: a loud clatter, followed by a muffled curse. We emerged back into the basement just in time to see a flash of someone dressed in dirty camouflage pants and a dark green shirt disappear up the stairs. We pursued, but we were too late. We managed to make it back to the servants' room just in time to see the back door swing closed.

Whoever it was had escaped.

EIGHT

There's gotta be something in here we can use to ID this guy," I began. I started pointing at various items in the perp's concealed underground lair. "Look, there's a shoddy-looking mattress over there. There's a bundle of dirty clothes in that corner. There's gotta be some of the guy's DNA on it."

Vance nodded. "I've already collected a few things and sent them off to the lab. But, based on the condition of the things we found, I'm not sure if the lab boys will find anything useful on it."

"Oh! Look here! I think you might be able to use this."

Vance and I turned at Jillian's exclamation. She was holding an old cigar case, and, as we neared, she held it out so we could see what was in it. There was a worn toothbrush.

"Way to go!" Vance praised, as he pulled out an evidence bag from his jacket pocket. He carefully dropped the toothbrush inside the baggie, sealed it, and noted it in his ever-present notebook. Then, just as he was straightening, he grunted once and reached inside the box. "Well, well, look what we have here. Looks like you were right, Zack. Check this out."

Toothpaste. And, it was some type of mint flavor. Vance carefully uncapped the tube and looked at the green goo. He held it out to me.

"Look familiar?"

"Why in the world would that dumbass brush his teeth in the sink?" I wondered aloud.

"Look around here, buddy. Maybe living down here was getting to him and he wanted some fresh air."

"Or," Jillian slowly began, "more likely, he's been using the bathroom this whole time and, just this once, forgot to clean up after himself."

That sobered me. I didn't know who this guy was, but one thing I *did* know was that I wanted him caught. Like, yesterday. Hopefully with the samples we've collected, an identification would be forthcoming.

"Man, this keeps getting better and better."

I turned back to Vance.

"What? Did you find something else?"

"I'll say," Vance commented, as he held up something in his gloved hand. "It's a razor. Between Jillian's toothbrush and this razor, I'm certain we have enough to ID our guy."

"That's assuming he's already in your system," I reminded my detective friend.

Vance shrugged. "True."

He bagged the razor and then disappeared up the

tunnel. While he was gone, I continued to lead the dogs around the perimeter of the second basement, only they seemed disinterested in anything else. Ten minutes later, Vance was back.

"Those two items are on their way to the lab," he reported. "I had them put a rush on it. Thanks to that bag of pins, there, this has now become a homicide investigation and that perp is our prime suspect."

I nodded, as I was only partially listening to him explain how DNA identification worked. I kept glancing around the confines of this small, smelly subterranean room. Someone had spent an inordinate amount of time living here. Why? Were they that desperate to lay their hands on Dame Highland's jewelry?

Then I remembered the *Czarina's Tear*. If what Jillian had said was true, then it meant that chicken-egg sized jewel could be worth millions of dollars. Tens of millions. That, unfortunately, was enough motivation to make someone willingly live in conditions such as this. The question I had now, was just how long had this squatter been living down here?

"What's on your mind?" Vance asked.

I shrugged and pointed back toward the tunnel.

"Let's get out of here, okay? The crime scene techs have already gone through this place. Sherlock and Watson have given it their once-over. This place gives me the creeps."

Vance nodded and, surprisingly, held out a hand. Not too certain what he was expecting, I hesitated.

"Give me one of the dogs. That tunnel is narrow. The last thing I want to have to write up is a civilian hurt themselves on my watch."

"Hardy ha ha."

"I'm serious. Give me Sherlock."

Bemused, and curious, I handed his leash to Vance. Sherlock, noticing the change of ownership of his leash, shook himself, snorted once, and promptly headed for the tunnel.

"There are times I'm convinced that they'll follow anyone," I said, as we carefully picked our way back to the first basement.

"I'm pretty sure he's hoping for another biscuit," Vance remarked, from up ahead. "Don't worry, boy. I've got you covered."

Just as we made it back inside the primary basement, Vance's cell rang. I watched Vance look at the display, cringe, give the two of us an apologetic look, and then hand Sherlock's leash to Jillian. He then hurried outside and, moments later, his car pulled away.

"I wonder what that was all about," Jillian said.

"I don't know. Hopefully, everything is okay."

"Zachary, I don't like knowing someone has been using this house without my knowledge *or* my permission."

"I know you don't," I soothed, as I wrapped my arms around her. I caught sight of Sherlock eyeing Jillian and waggled a finger at him. "We'll catch this guy. I promise."

Sherlock woofed just then, as if to say he promised, too. Or else as a warning: *get your hands off my daddy!* I'm not sure which.

Jillian smiled, but then frowned as Sherlock let out a second woof. Moments later, the hackles on Watson's back stood up. Both dogs, I might add, were craning their necks to look up above our heads.

I took Jillian's hand as she wrapped Sherlock's leash tightly around her wrist.

"Sorry, boy. You're not getting away from me. I've seen what you've pulled on your daddy."

"True story," I muttered, as the four of us hurried up the stairs.

We emerged back in the servants' room. Both corgis were pulling on their leash, eager to head toward the foyer. Uncertain of what to expect, I managed to snag a small crowbar along the way. Hefting it like a caveman holding his club, we rounded the corner and approached the front door. What did we find?

Nothing.

"What's the deal, guys?" I asked, as I looked down at the dogs. However, my irritation rapidly dissipated as I saw them looking at the front door. "You want to go outside? Oh, I get it. You want to follow Vance, is that it?"

Allowing the dogs to lead the way, we headed outside, but were still rewarded with absolutely nothing. Nada. Zip.

I heard Watson whine. That's when I noticed both dogs were staring suspiciously at the surrounding vegetation, as though our perp was hiding nearby. I swallowed nervously. Could it be possible? That rare garnet had a huge price tag associated with it. It might be too tempting to give up altogether.

I grasped Jillian's hand tightly in my own.

"Come on. We're calling it a day."

"It's not even noon," Jillian pointed out.

"True, but it'll give me time to check with the locksmith. I want to be certain this place is as secure as we can make it."

Jillian gave me a peck on my cheek.

"Thank you, Zachary."

* * *

Eureka! It had taken just under two days for the PVPD's lab to be able to pull some DNA off either the toothbrush or the razor and identify it. And, luck was on our side. We had a name!

Curtis Stiller.

And, as Vance informed me, our friend Mr. Stiller had a rap sheet that was longer than my arm. Let's see, where should I start? Well, he has a history of petty theft, which fits in with what this jerk has been doing. There was also four counts of grand theft auto. Now that I think about it, I really should have asked Jillian what happened to Dame Highland's car. We were told it was her pride and joy. Why the *Czarina's Tear* didn't hold that distinction, I will never know. But, there was no mention of the car anywhere. For all I knew, the two perps who killed Dame Highland probably made off in it and then sold it.

As I read through the report on this Stiller guy, I came across a *possession of stolen goods* entry. I snorted. Well, that wouldn't be a surprise. Amused, I made it through another dozen entries when a thought occurred.

Possession of stolen goods?

I quickly returned to the theft entry again and read the particulars. It said here that Curtis Stiller was busted for possession of stolen goods last year, in Portland. Apparently, he had been fencing stolen antiques. If Mr. Stiller was otherwise occupied with stripping Highland House of its valuables, then wouldn't those pawned antiques belong to Jillian?

I texted Vance and asked him about the possession of stolen goods charge on Curtis' rap sheet. I wanted to know should any of the stolen antiques be recovered, seeing how they probably came from Highland House, would they be returned to Jillian? Vance promptly texted back and said he'd begin the process of trying to recover any stolen items.

By the time I had sent the second text, complete with two full paragraphs of questions and observations, my fingers were tired. How kids nowadays could continuously tap out conversations by the hour eluded me. Wouldn't it be simpler to just call the person? I mean, you *are* holding a phone, right?

"What's the matter, Zack? Are your fingers tired?"

"Bite me, pal. I can only text for so long. I figured it'd be easier this way."

"Did you notice a pattern to Stiller's crimes?" Vance suddenly asked.

"A pattern? No. What kind of pattern are you talking about?"

"Everything he had been busted for, during the last five years or so, more than likely involved that house. I mean, look at his rap sheet. Breaking and entering. Aggravated assault. Petty theft. Possession of stolen goods. Zack, it looks like our friend Curtis has been at it now for years."

"I can believe it," I decided. "You saw the condition of the second basement. If I didn't know any better, I'd say he dug that tunnel and excavated that space below the real basement himself."

"That's an interesting theory, buddy."

"It just came to me," I admitted.

"I'm glad you called," my detective friend said. "It's been two days, and I was planning on checking in with you today. I wanted to let you know that I have a feeling Curtis is still in the area."

"I believe that, too. I think he has too much riding in that house to give up now."

"Exactly. For that reason, I've stationed a car outside Jillian's new house until this guy is caught, and…"

"Do you really think he's stupid enough to try something?" I interrupted.

"And you don't? As I was saying, there'll be a car outside the house, and an APB has already been issued. This is a small town. He'll turn up eventually."

"Do we have a picture of the guy?"

"We do. I'm sending it to your phone."

Right on cue, my phone chirped. Yeah, I know. Phones don't chirp. Well, long story short, mine does. Someone changed my text alert a while back, and even though I have long since figured out how to revert it back, I kind of like it. Now that I know what to listen for, the strange alert can stay.

"Well," I said, as I gazed at the picture looking up at me from my phone's display, "I can honestly say I've never seen him before."

The picture showed a gaunt, dark-haired man who could have been anywhere from his mid-twenties up into his early forties. The face staring back at me had seen some hard times, no doubt about it. And, unfortunately, there was also a look of determination in his haggard appearance. This was someone who has gone through hell, and was fully prepared to ride out the storm if it meant he'd get what he wanted. I thought of Jillian and immediately frowned. There was no way I was going to let this joker anywhere near that house again. Somehow, we had to find a way to catch this guy.

"Show Jillian."

"And how do you know we're together?"

"Please. The two of you are always together. I'm willing to bet this Friday's choice of restaurants that you're presently in Cookbook Nook."

Dammit. I wasn't that predictable, was I? As much as I didn't want Vance to be able to choose the restaurant for this week's Friday Night Get Together, I wasn't about to take him up on that bet.

"Lucky guess, pal. And it's no deal."

Vance laughed.

"Hi, Vance!" Jillian smoothly cut in.

"Hey, Jillian. We were just talking about you."

"Oh? Nice things, I hope."

"With Zack? Of course. He always has something nice to say about you. That is, unless it's about your choice of movies at…"

"Hey, Jillian!" I smoothly interrupted. "Did you see that Vance's video is about to break four million views? Would you like to help it hit that record?"

"Okay, okay. Anyway, would you look at the picture I just sent Zack? I'd like to know if he looks familiar to you."

"Certainly. Zachary, give me your phone. Let's see. Hmm, I'm sorry. I don't know any Stillers, nor have I ever seen this man before."

"And you're supposed to know everyone in town," I teased.

"I do," Jillian insisted. She held my phone up in a questioning manner. "And what does that suggest to you?"

"That our guy is not from around here," Vance answered for me.

"Exactly," Jillian agreed.

"He may not be from around here," I argued, "but

he clearly has been here a while. If you don't recognize him, Jillian, then that could only mean this guy keeps a low profile. He doesn't want anyone to know he's in town."

"I'm going to share this guy's picture with the guys here at the precinct," Vance was saying. "That way, if Curtis slips up, we might be able to spot him."

Jillian was nodding. "That's not a bad idea. I'll do the same."

"I'd rather you didn't," Vance began. "Leave this to us, Jillian."

"You have your people look for him, and I'll do the same," Jillian was saying. "Besides, my network of friends is way more extensive than your small handful of police officers in your address book."

"She's got you there," I chuckled.

"Fine. Just promise me something: if you get word that our perp has been spotted, do not confront him, okay? Observe only. The only thing we want to know is if he's still in the area."

"Which we figure he is," I added.

"Exactly."

"Well, if this person is still in Pomme Valley," Jillian said, "then the whole town will be our eyes and ears."

"I'll bet your people find him before his will," I idly commented.

"Not a chance, pal. We're the professionals here."

"Would you like to place a wager on that, detective?" Jillian sweetly asked.

Vance fell silent. I had to lean forward and tap the screen on my phone to make certain the call hadn't been dropped.

"Still there, pal? Want to make this interesting?"

"Umm... what'd you have in mind?"

"Well..." I began.

"Not you. Jillian."

"Oh, you're going to regret that," Jillian slyly said. "I guarantee you I can come up with a more, let's say, *meaningful* wager than Zack."

"I strongly doubt that, but you're on. Let's hear the stakes."

"If I, or any of my contacts, spots Mr. Stiller first, then I win. If your officers locates him first, then you win."

"And the stakes?"

"If I win, then you will accompany me and Zack to Chateau Restaurant & Wine Bar ..."

"Huh? That's no penalty for me. I agree. And if I win..."

"You didn't let me finish," Jillian interrupted. "You will accompany us to my favorite restaurant, where *I* will pick up the tab. No, Zachary, don't argue. I will pick up the tab, and you, Mr. Samuelson, will order the frog legs."

The biggest grin I was capable of giving anyone appeared on my face. I mouthed *Awesome!* to my girlfriend and waited to hear what dear Vance had to say about the matter.

"Ummm..."

Jillian pulled out her phone and began texting like a pro.

"I'm impressed, Vance," Jillian exclaimed. "I thought for certain you would have had a more adverse reaction to learning you'd be eating frog legs. Good for you."

"Ummm..."

"Look at that! I just heard from Tori. She's on board. She can't wait to see you try frog legs, either, especially after giving Zachary such a hard time after he mistakenly ordered them."

"But…"

"Good. It's settled. Now, what happens if you win the wager?"

"Wait. What just happened here?"

"You just agreed to eat frog legs should a civilian locate our perp before your people do," I smoothly explained. "And, just so we understand one another, I plan on making a follow-up viral hit with you: Detective forced to choke down frog legs. I should be able to hit a million plus hits with that, easy."

"Dang it, Zack, you stay out of this. All right. I have faith in my people. I'm going to win this wager, so what do I have to lose, right?"

Jillian smiled, leaned forward, and set her elbows on the table next to the phone.

"I'm waiting."

"All right. If you lose, then you should have to eat something you wouldn't want to, as well."

"Like what?"

"Zack? What doesn't she like to eat?"

"Oh, no. Leave me out of this."

"It's okay, Zachary," Jillian assured me. "You can help him out."

"No repercussions?" I suspiciously asked.

"None. I enjoy most food."

Jillian's phone beeped and she typed out another message. Presumably to Tori.

I muted the call and looked at my girlfriend.

"How certain are you that your team will find him first?"

"Unquestionably."

"All right. I know what to suggest which will get him to agree to this. I personally can't wait to see him eat frog legs."

"What do you have in mind?"

I unmuted the call.

"Vance, still with me?"

"Yes. What did you do? Did you mute the call? What were you saying to Jillian?"

"She doesn't like spicy food. The steak house we like to go to has spicy hot wings. I could smell them as someone near our table ordered them. Trust me, they're hot. Have her eat some of those."

"Jillian? Is he telling the truth?"

"He is," Jillian sadly confirmed. Her face set as she stared at me. "All right. I agree to those terms, but with one addendum. Should I lose, Zack will be eating those wings with me."

I groaned. Should've seen that one coming.

"Fine," I sighed. "I accept."

Jillian smiled. "Good. Then it's all settled."

"You will be eating those spicy hot wings," Vance gloated. "And I will be there to document the whole thing. Let's see how you enjoy being a viral sensation."

"Except, it'll be you eating the frog legs," Jillian suddenly announced. "Mr. Stiller was seen at the Hardware store two weeks ago, and four days ago, he paid a visit to Bella's Baubles."

"What?!"

Jillian held her phone out to me so I could verify the news.

"It's true," I confirmed, as I read the text message from

one of her friends. "It says here he purchased duct tape, rope, and heavy-duty bolt cutters. That doesn't sound very good."

"No, it doesn't," Vance agreed. "What about the jewelry store? What was he doing there?"

"I was about to call Isabella and find out."

"Don't you think that's something I should do?"

"Have you received official word Curtis Stiller has been spotted?" Jillian asked.

"Er, no."

"I'll find out what he was doing there and then I'll call you back."

"Umm, okay. Thanks, Jillian."

"I suggest a bottle of ketchup," I added.

"Huh?"

"For your frog legs. It might hide the flavor."

"Bite me, Zack."

Isabella MacKenzie, Jillian later told me, was the owner of Bella's Baubles. I could say that it's the only jewelry store in Pomme Valley, but you probably know that by now. This town isn't big enough to have more than one type of store in competition with another. So, that's why you've heard me say there's only one jewelry store in town, or one pet store in town, or the only locksmith in town, and so on. With the exception of our meager selection of restaurants, that's how the townsfolk preferred it: small and quaint. Seeing how the town council agreed, I don't think it likely that any changes will be coming our way any time soon.

As I was saying, Isabella MacKenzie owned Bella's Baubles. Well, she and Richard, her husband. She was a cheerful woman in her late fifties who treated her customers as though she was running a Mom and Pop grocery store.

If a customer didn't have the funds to make a purchase, then the honor system kicked in and the MacKenzies would trust the customer to pay whenever they could.

I found it hard to believe that a business which placed so much trust with their patrons would thrive, but strangely enough, it did. People loved the store. It was always busy, and Isabella always had a smile for you, regardless of the mood you happened to be in.

"Thank you for calling Bella's Baubles. This is Isabella. How can I help you today?"

"Hi, Bella, it's Jillian."

"Jillian! I can't say I'm surprised. Once I received your text, and saw the picture of the person you were looking for, I knew that man was up to no good. Richard, didn't I say he was up to no good?"

Both Jillian and I could hear a male voice grunt in the background.

"Richard agrees," Bella translated.

"Can you tell us what he was doing there?" Jillian asked.

"He wanted Richard to give an appraisal."

"On a piece of jewelry?" I asked, growing angry.

It could only mean that PV's Public Enemy #1 had located some of Dame Highland's missing collection, but how? And why now? Sensing my frustration, Jillian placed a hand over mine.

"Did he have the piece with him, or was he simply asking about it?"

"Oh, heaven's no. He didn't have the piece. I think he knew it would arouse too many suspicions."

"He found something," I grumbled.

"It's possible," Jillian whispered.

"I can tell you, with certainty, he didn't have the piece

he was asking about," Isabella's voice interjected.

"How can you be so certain?" I wanted to know.

"Because he asked what Richard knew about Siberian emeralds."

Siberian emeralds? This was news to me. For a second there, I was worried Curtis Stiller had been asking about the *Czarina's Tear*.

"I'm not familiar with Siberian emeralds," Jillian admitted. "I take it they're from Russia? Are they valuable?"

"Highly valuable," Richard's voice said, in the background.

Sorry. I should have explained. Isabella ran the store. Richard was the licensed jeweler.

"Rare?" I asked.

"Very," Richard admitted.

"I wonder if Dame Highland had any of those," I quietly whispered.

Jillian shrugged.

"What did he want to know about them?" I asked, as I leaned closer to the phone. "Aside from price, that is. Did he say anything else?"

"Only that he expected to be getting his hands on a prime stone and wanted to know how easy it would be to sell."

Just then, Jillian's phone beeped. She was receiving another call. We both glanced at the display and saw that Robert was calling. I mentally crossed my fingers and hoped Jillian wasn't about to receive some bad news.

"Isabella? I have someone on the other line. Can I call you back?"

"If it's easier," I hastily interjected, "I can come down there and talk with you in person."

"Sure! I'd be delighted, Zachary. On one condition."

"And what would that be?" I cautiously asked.

"That you bring those adorable dogs with you."

"Ah. Not a problem. I'll see you shortly, Mrs. MacKenzie."

Jillian nodded her approval, ended the call, and hastily switched over to Robert's.

"Robert? I'm here. What's going on?"

"I'm sorry to bother you, Ms. Cooper. It's nothing serious. One of my guys located what could only be described as a secret room and I wanted to let you know about it."

"In the master bedroom closet?" Jillian asked. "We already found it, but thank you for letting me know. Wait. Are you talking about the big room at the northeastern corner of the first floor? Or, maybe you're referring to the den, which is the room adjacent to the game room?"

"There are hidden rooms in all those places?" Robert incredulously asked.

"They're everywhere in there," I confirmed.

"Hello, Mr. Anderson," Robert's voice said. "But I was referring to what we found in the basement."

"The second basement, accessible through that tunnel in the back of the wardrobe?" I asked. "I thought you knew about it."

"No, señor. I'm talking about what was hidden by the pool table."

Surprised, I met Jillian's eyes, "That's a new one on us, Robert."

Jillian nodded, as if she had come to a decision.

"Tell you what. I'll be right there, Robert. Zachary? Will you be okay talking to Isabella without me?"

"She isn't Clara Hanson, so I'll be fine."

Clara Hanson was the owner of A Lazy Afternoon, PV's local bookstore. She was a nice enough elderly woman, only she didn't believe in personal space and she … how do I say this in a politically correct fashion? She is single, and I do believe she's ready to mingle. Enough said? I try to avoid her at all costs. Isabella MacKenzie, though, was a calm, collected breeze when compared to the hurricane that was Clara.

"I'll be fine. I'll go get the dogs and we'll be on our way. Let me know if you find anything good at the house, okay?"

"I will, Zachary."

Thirty minutes later, I was seated on the customer-side of the counter at Bella's Baubles. Husband and wife team Richard and Isabella sat opposite me. Well, Isabella was. Richard had retreated to his little booth where he worked on minor repairs, which happened to be less than five feet from us. Dozens and dozens of tiny tools, tweezers, loupes, and so forth, rested in neat rows on their respective shelves.

"Tell me, Zachary," Isabella was saying, as she knelt down to give each of the corgis a few treats. I recognized the bag as being from Farmhouse Bakery, and knew they were Sherlock and Watson's favorite goodie: bagel bits. "Why is there so much interest about Siberian emeralds all of a sudden? Yes, those gems are highly coveted, but those stones are usually no larger than four or five carats."

"One to two," Richard corrected, without looking up from his work on a golden watch with a jeweled band.

"One to two," Isabella corrected. "And what do you know about this man? Was I right? Was he up to no good?"

I was facing a conundrum. I wasn't too sure how much to divulge to the MacKenzies. Do I tell them that Curtis Stiller had been illegally squatting in Highland House for years, hoping to get his hands on Dame Hilda Highland's long-missing jewelry? And what about the *Czarina's Tear*?

Something wasn't adding up. Curtis had been inside this shop, asking about prices for a prime stone he was hoping to get his hands on. He had to be talking about Highland House, but what stone was he talking about? What did this little punk know that we didn't?

"These Siberian emeralds," I began, "do they go by any other names?"

"A few," Richard answered. "They are mainly known by their trade names: Siberian chrysolites, or Ural chrysolites."

"Still haven't heard of 'em," I said, shaking my head.

"But," Richard continued, keeping his eyes firmly pressed to his jeweler's microscope and performing surgery on a couple of gems embedded in the watch band, "everyone recognizes them by their official name: demantoid garnet."

Well, I'll be a monkey's uncle. I should have seen that coming.

"Did you tell this guy that Siberian emeralds were also known as demantoid garnets?" I asked.

"I did, yes. Did I do something wrong?"

"Not at all, Isabella. I was just curious what this guy has been up to. I wonder what this prime stone is that he's been asking about."

"He seemed to think it'd be worth a fortune," Isabella recalled. "Then I told him if he could provide provenance for the stone, it'd be worth twice as much."

"More like triple, or possibly quadruple, depending on

the history of the stone," Richard added, from his booth.

"Provenance?" I repeated, puzzled. "What's that?"

"It's a history of ownership for a prized piece of art," Isabella explained. "Or, in this case, jewelry. Let's say, for example, you found an emerald ring with a five-carat diamond. Depending on quality, it could range anywhere from $7,500 to $15,000. Please bear in mind that these prices vary on a daily basis, based on current market value."

I nodded.

"Continuing on, let's say it was rumored that Queen Elizabeth II of England once owned the ring *and* wore it. Those rumors alone would probably double it in price. Wouldn't you agree, Richard?"

Richard wordlessly nodded.

"Now, if documentation was produced which undoubtedly proved that the queen did, in fact, own the ring, and let's say it was given as a present to someone, well, that one bit of proof would fetch a price considerably higher than its normal value."

"I get it. Provide proof and it's worth more money."

"A crude analogy, but accurate, none the less."

My cell phone rang. Jillian's lovely face appeared on my phone's display.

"Hi, Jillian. Is everything okay?"

"Yes, it is!"

Was it me, or did Jillian sound excited?

"Are you done at Isabella's? If so, please come over here. Hurry!"

"What's going on?" I asked, growing alarmed.

"Zachary, I found a necklace. It has diamonds in it!"

NINE

They said those were real diamonds," I said to Jillian, sometime later. "Real diamonds, and Richard even said the blue ones were diamonds, too, although that doesn't make any sense to me."

"Diamonds can come in other colors," Jillian reminded me. "Blue happens to be a rare color, for a diamond. That's why Richard appraised this necklace the way he did."

"He said it was easily worth more than $60,000," I recalled. "For something that, at first glance, looks as though it could be costume jewelry."

"You say that only because it's hard to believe these stones are real, and not glass."

I nodded. "True."

A lot has happened in the last hour. I had quickly

driven over to Highland House to see for myself what Jillian had found. In this case, it was a very expensive diamond necklace. A blue and white diamond necklace, if you want to get technical. I had originally refused to believe the necklace contained real gemstones, so we took the necklace to have it appraised by a jeweler in town. I mean, there were so many stones, and all of them were real? No wonder it had appraised for so high. And, there were more blue diamonds than the standard white. Er, clear, I guess. What I had first thought to be a normal, blue tear drop necklace has turned out to be so much more. My only thought at this point was, could this be something that was owned by Dame Highland? It had to be! Who else could have afforded something like this back in the 1920's and '30s?

"Did you catch the part about the necklace being platinum?" I asked Jillian, as we drove through town.

Jillian nodded. "I did. Why do you think we're on our way to the bank? I don't want to keep something this valuable inside my house, thank you very much. I'd rather not attract unwarranted attention, either."

I nodded. "Couldn't agree more. Hey, have you ever heard of something called provenance?"

"Of course. It's a record of ownership for an antique. It can be used for paintings, sculpture, and jewelry. Provenance is used as a guide for authenticating and quality."

"That sounds like a text book definition," I chuckled.

"Because it is," Jillian admitted. "I know where you're going with this, Zachary. You're hoping to find some proof that Dame Highland once owned this necklace, aren't you?"

"Guilty as charged. And, believe it or not, I really don't

care what it does to its value. I'm just curious to know if we're on the right track. Did you actually find one of Dame Highland's missing pieces of jewelry? That's what I want to know. That sure was a lucky break. Er, no pun intended."

Jillian giggled, "I know, right? They were preparing to replace the burnt wiring, which meant they had to strip paneling and sheet rock away from the walls. The den has several bookcases in it. Who would've thought that one of those bookcases had a secret drawer hidden within the decorative panel on the top of that bookcase? Not me."

"That bookcase didn't have any books on it, did it? I think I remember seeing them empty when we were there last weekend."

"It was empty," Jillian confirmed. "All three were, in that room. Most people would have thought to hide the necklace in one of the books, I'm sure. I never would have imagined it'd be possible to conceal a sixty-thousand-dollar necklace within the bookcase itself."

"I thought Robert was going to throttle that worker," I said, as I pulled into the bank parking lot. "I could see it in that guy's eyes. He was grateful you came to his rescue."

"If it wasn't for him, I would never have found this. All right, would you wait right here? I'll be back as soon as I can."

"We're not going anywhere," I assured her.

Ten minutes later, we were off, only we weren't headed home and, for once, we weren't headed to Highland House. Where were we going? Well, Jillian must have been thinking the same thing I had been thinking: if that necklace *did* belong to Dame Highland, and she deliberately hid it in a piece of furniture, then what were the chances that she had hidden other bits of jewelry in other pieces of furniture?

She had immediately suggested we head to the storage unit she had rented to find out. Located on the western side of town, adjacent to *Rupert's Gas & Auto*, we parked in front of the office. I waited with the dogs while Jillian checked in with the manager.

Jillian emerged, holding the key to her unit. Yes, I know most people would simply carry a copy of the key with them. However, Jillian left hers with the front desk. I will also point out that she gave me a copy of the key, too, just so she'd have a backup.

"That was odd," Jillian began, as we walked companionably toward her 10' x 25' unit.

"What was?" I wanted to know, as I took the key from her, unlocked the padlock, and rolled the door up.

"Steve. He's the manager here. He wanted to know if I had talked to Vinnie yet."

"Who?" I asked.

"Vince Rupert."

I hooked a thumb behind me.

"Rupert, from Rupert's Gas & Auto?"

"The very same."

"Why would he be trying to reach you?"

"I'm not sure. From what Steve tells me, Vinnie has been over here a number of times since I had rented the storage unit, wanting to know if he knew when I'd be back next."

"He wants to talk to you face to face, and not on the phone," I guessed.

"It seems that way. If he wants to talk, then that's fine. He just has to call me. Okay, here we are."

I gazed at the furniture removed from Highland House for the first time. Right off the bat, I could see that the furniture had been professionally handled and stowed. How did I know that? Because all the various pieces were covered with heavy quilted blankets and then it looked as though they were shrink-wrapped. I experimentally poked a finger at a blanket-covered item that had the right shape for a grandfather clock. It wasn't shrink-wrap, but more like a heavy-duty Saran wrap.

"This is gonna be a problem," I mused aloud, as I looked at all the pieces of furniture that were residing within the storage unit. "Look at them. Whoever you hired to move them did a fine job, that's for sure."

"Well, maybe we could unwrap one or two and see if there's anything unusual about it?" Jillian suggested.

I shrugged. "Sure. We can do that. Where would you like to start?"

Jillian turned and pointed at the closest object, which was what I had thought of as the grandfather clock.

"We can start with this one. Here. Help me find the edge. That way, we can re-wrap this once we're done."

Instead of trying to describe to you how difficult that was, namely unwrapping something that had been bound in heavy duty cling wrap, let me bring up another analogy. Have you ever used a packing-tape gun? Has the tape ever slipped out of its guide and adhered itself back to the roll? Do you remember how long it took to try and find the end, only to end up scratching at the surface of the roll for what felt like hours, with no progress? Now, take that and multiply it by ten. It was all I could do to not jam my fingers through the infernal stuff and simply yank that clingy wrap away.

"This stuff sure does stick to itself," Jillian observed. "I thought I had found a ... ah. There it is. Just a moment.

I think I have it."

Moments later, we were unwrapping a great sheet of the wrapping material, and trying our darnedest not to let it touch itself, lest it render the whole sheet useless. Laughing and cursing, we managed to drape the sheet over several nearby chairs. Jillian then carefully peeled away the packing quilts and we observed the antique piece of furniture.

I was right. It was a grandfather's clock. A 5-tube Colonial, if you wanted to get technical. Jillian gingerly inspected the finials at the top of the clock. She opened the upper door and carefully shone her light on it (her phone's LED light, that is). She ran her fingers along the carved overlay. Then she opened the lower door and inspected the weights, the pulley system, and even the five tubes that were responsible for producing the clock's tones. Lastly, she knelt on the ground so she could run her fingers along the toe molding.

Nothing.

"Would you care to try?" Jillian asked me.

I looked down at the corgis. Both had sunk into *down* positions and were watching Jillian's clock inspection as though they were watching television. However, at no point in time had they given the slightest bit of attention to anything the two of us had done in this unit. Quite frankly, I think they were bored.

"I trust you. You did a great job. Let's wrap this thing back up and try something else."

The next piece we unwrapped turned out to be a child's doll dresser with four drawers. It also had one of those old-fashioned flip mirrors on top of it. Jillian poked and prodded the entire thing before finally giving up. She looked at me and shrugged helplessly.

"I really thought we were on to something. I thought, if Dame Highland was clever enough to conceal a valuable diamond necklace in something as trivial as a bookcase, then she more than likely hid the rest of her jewelry in the other pieces of furniture."

"It's a good theory," I agreed. "But, what if this Curtis guy has been locating various pieces and selling them?"

"But nothing has turned up!" Jillian protested.

"That we know of," I reminded her. "Not all pawn brokers are reputable and honest. For that matter, we don't even know if whoever he sold them to knows their full value."

"That's assuming Mr. Stiller found more of her jewelry *and* sold it."

I thought about it for a moment and then shook my head.

"No, I think you're right. If he learned there was a chance jewelry could have been hidden inside the furniture, he would have long ago destroyed every last stick of it in that house."

"That's a good point, Zachary. Well, where would you like to go from here? I don't think we will find anything useful in here. I'm sorry for dragging you out here."

"Don't worry about it. Let's go back to Highland House. There's still furniture in there. One of the guys found another hidden room. I'll bet you the answer is there. We just have to find it."

I have gone on record numerous times, stating that I am oftentimes wrong, frequently really wrong, and on a few times, horribly wrong. It certainly felt like the last one to me. Jillian and I searched that house from top to bottom. No, we didn't discover any more hidden rooms. The dogs seemed to perk up whenever we went upstairs, but I think it was because they loved to jump up on the huge king bed in the master bedroom and watch the door. Personally, I think it was because the bed was lower to the ground.

Anyway, whenever Jillian and I would head off to explore another room in the house, if the dogs ever wandered off, we'd always find them in the master bedroom. Now, I know what you're thinking. There must be something Sherlock and Watson want us to find in there. And, it's a possibility the two of us discussed several times. However, no amount of searching in there could uncover anything we didn't already know. I simply could not figure out why they were so fascinated with this one room. More specifically, the big bas-relief thingamajig on the southern wall. I must have stared at that blasted thing for hours, and had nothing to show for it.

I found Jillian sitting on the bed several hours later, with the dogs, as I returned after searching the second basement. It was creepy as hell down there and I wasn't about to subject Jillian to that again if she didn't have to. I sat down heavily on the bed and eyed my girlfriend. Well, I eyed all three of them. And, for the record, all three were now staring directly at me.

"Find anything?" Jillian wearily asked.

"Not a darn thing, I'm afraid."

"I'd say it's about time we call it quits here. I know it's early, but I was thinking about doing a little research in the library. Would you care to join me?"

"I would be delighted. If I don't have to go up and down several flights of steps, then I'm your guy."

"No steps," Jillian confirmed. "What about you two? Care to go with us?"

Both dogs jumped down to the ground, but not before Sherlock turned to look back at the bed. Curious, I glanced at Jillian before looking back at Sherlock. What was the deal with the bed? Was there something under it?

I passed the leashes to Jillian.

"Keep an eye on these two, would you? I want to see what's under this thing."

Jillian led the dogs to the other side of the room and waited while I tipped the mattress over on its side so I could see underneath it. Nothing. I then pulled the box spring out of the sleigh bed frame and also inspected the undersides. Again, nothing. Grumbling, I was in the process of lowering the mattress back into position when I hesitated.

Something was on the ground, about to be covered up by the mattress. It was small, dark, and almost blended in with the dark gray carpeting in the room. Grunting with surprise, I tipped the box spring back up on its side and rested it against the wall. Stretching over the frame, I reached down to retrieve that which had caught my eye.

"What is it?" Jillian wanted to know.

I turned and held out my hand.

"It's a cube."

"A cube? A cube of what?"

I brought my hand close to my face and studied the one-inch by one-inch dark gray object. The surface was dotted with tiny holes, and on one of the sides there was a teeny tiny button. Curious, I pressed it. I waited for a few moments and then grunted. Nothing happened. I walked over to Jillian and let her take the cube from my hand.

"This looks like a speaker," Jillian decided.

I stared at the tiny cube.

"That? You think that's a speaker?"

Jillian nodded. "I do. We can test this. Would you hold the leashes, please?"

Once control of the dogs had been returned to me, Jillian reached into her purse for her cell. She tapped the screen a few times before looking expectantly at the tiny device. She frowned, and then shrugged.

"I thought for sure this was a speaker. If it was, then more than likely it would have had a Bluetooth chip in it. If that was true, then my phone should be able to pick it up. However, it didn't find anything."

I remembered pressing the pinhole-sized button. I held a hand out. After Jillian passed the cube back, I pointed at her phone.

"Hang on a second. I want you to try again, but let me press this first."

Once I gave Jillian the signal, she tried again to search for any nearby Bluetooth devices. This time, her phone chirped and displayed a new entry: Micron Bluetooth Speaker. Jillian tapped the newly discovered device and was rewarded with a soft chime. Then, bringing up her list of songs on her phone, she hit Play.

The sounds of *Uptown Funk* filled the room with surprising clarity. A look of anger passed over her features. She pointed at the cube.

"Curtis has been using this to play eerie sounds, hasn't he? It's so small that I bet it was taped under that mattress."

I turned back to the mattress and examined the surface. Sure enough, there was a strip of beige two-sided tape near the end of the bed. Being light brown to begin with, the tape blended in almost perfectly with the rest of the mattress, so even if you were looking for it, you'd be hard-pressed to spot it.

"You're right. There's some adhesive residue right here. Good job, Sherlock! Okay. You, too, Watson. I'm sorry. I don't have any Scooby snacks for you. We'd need Vance for that."

"Scooby snacks?" Jillian repeated, with a giggle.

"He always has doggie biscuits with him," I reminded her. "What else would you call them?"

"I wonder how many more of these there are around here," Jillian said. "If the cubes are turned on, which I presume they are, then our phones should be able to spot them. Should we look for them?"

Shaking my head, I was about ready to throw the device away when I thought better of it and dropped it back on the ground. Confused, Jillian stared at the small speaker.

"What did you do that for? Shouldn't we get rid of it?"

"Then he'll know we found it," I pointed out.

"He already knows we know he's here," Jillian argued. "I think that speaker is a moot point right about now."

"Still, I'd rather not disturb them. We've already touched this one, but if you're right, there are others in the house. I say we let Vance and his guys find them. That way, they can check for prints. Besides, I think our pal Curtis is going to come back. We just have to figure out how to catch him."

Jillian wandered over to the closest window and looked outside.

"For all we know, he's already out there, somewhere, watching us right now. He's probably just waiting for us to leave."

I pointed at the marked squad car parked just outside the front door.

"Not with the police just outside. Oh, don't get me wrong, I think he's trying to figure out how to get back inside, but as long as Vance has our backs, I think we're okay."

Jillian took my hand, "Come on. We still have an hour before the library closes. I'd like to see if there's anything on file about that necklace I found. It would be wonderful if we could find some type of proof that it belonged to Hilda."

"I think we both know it belonged to Hilda," I argued. "However, you're right. Let's find proof. Out of curiosity, if we do, what do you plan on doing with it? Are you going to sell it?"

"Probably not," Jillian decided. "I might loan it to our museum here in town. I'll see if they're interested in setting up an exhibit about this house and Dame Hilda. As we've already learned, this house has quite a history."

"Sherlock? Watson? Come on. We're going for a ride."

"Should we take them home?" Jillian asked.

"No, they should be fine. It's been a perfect day outside, weather-wise. They'll be fine in the Jeep. Besides, I keep a bag of treats in there. They should be okay for a little while."

Half an hour later, we were sitting at one of the terminals inside the PV library. Jillian, being much more adept on the library's computer system than me, was sitting in the chair and typing away. Every so often, she'd pull the catalog number to some book she'd want me to find. I'd find it, and then, together, we'd go through it, looking for any mention of the Highland name.

Jillian had been right. This library had a lot of information about one of its most colorful citizens. And, much to my delight, that included photos. Every single one of them, thank the lucky stars, was digital. When you think about it, it's actually very smart. That way, the library doesn't have to waste precious storage space in order to keep a physical copy there inside the building. Oh, I'm sure they still had the originals, but I was also pretty certain that they were tucked safely away in some storage facility.

Going through the photos, we saw pictures of Dame Highland in her early teenage years, next to whom I'm guessing was her father. Then we saw photo after photo of her in her car, the sporty-looking roadster we had seen in the album back in Highland House. Seriously, there had to be several dozen photographs of Dame Highland and that car, in various locales. There she was, driving up the coast on what I presumed was Highway 101. There she was, driving her car through Sequoia National Park.

"I wonder what type of car that is and where it is now," I mused aloud.

"I'm sure it's long gone," Jillian answered, as she scrolled through more photos. "Out of curiosity, why do you ask? Do you like it?"

I nodded. "I do. It reminds me of those old gangster movies. I always imagined Bugsy Malone owning a car like this. I wonder…"

I trailed off as a thought occurred. What if Dame Highland hid her jewels in her car? What do you suppose were the chances of tracking that car down after all these years?

"You wonder *what*?" Jillian asked, after she noticed I had trailed off.

"Could she have hidden anything in her car?"

Jillian shrugged. "Possibly. However, I don't think we'll

ever know. That car is long gone by now. Think about it. Hilda was murdered in 1947. That's over 70 years ago. Even if the car survived, it'd be nothing more than a rusted hulk by now."

"What a depressing thought," I muttered. "Hey, that picture shows promise. She's wearing some jewelry in it, at least."

Jillian nodded. "I found some files on another server. This one has a different batch of photos. Based on the upload date, they haven't been here that long."

"Just under two months, actually," a new voice said.

We both turned to see a young kid, probably in his late teens to early twenties, standing just behind us. Annoyed that this person was able to sneak up on us, I glanced at Jillian, but she was already smiling at the kid.

"And who are you?" I politely asked.

"Jason Merrick. I work here."

"Ah. Well, hello Jason. My name is…"

"You're Zack Anderson," Jason interrupted. "I know who you are, of course."

I narrowed my eyes, "Dare I ask *how* you know me? No offense, pal, but you don't look old enough to drink."

"I'm nineteen," Jason confirmed. "And no, I don't drink. Let's just say I'm an ardent admirer of your dogs. And, don't ask me how I know, but they're presently in your car. Is there any way I can go out and meet them?"

"You know the dogs are in my car?" I repeated, amazed. And, truthfully, a little creeped out. "And how would you know that? I'm not sure I like where this is going, kid."

"No! Oh, no! That's not what I meant at all. I've wanted to meet them for some time now, and now that you're here, I know they're close. Your dogs are adorable. That's all I'm trying to say."

"Focus, Jason," I told the kid. "You said that the pictures we're looking at were recently uploaded? Tell me how you know that and I'll personally take you out to my Jeep and make the introductions. Once we're done in here, that is."

"Because I'm the one who scanned them all in," Jason promptly told us. "What a job that was. Do you have any idea how long I spent scanning in those four boxes of pictures? All of them cropped and scanned at 300 DPI."

"DPI?" Jillian repeated.

"Dots Per Inch," Jason translated. "Just believe me when I say that I spent nearly a year on it."

"To scan in some pictures?" I asked, amazed.

"Well, it wasn't just those," Jason clarified. "I was tasked with clearing out our back room. We've been given lots of donations over the years. Then, me and my big mouth … I suggested we could clear up room if we digitize documents and photos. Guess who they asked to do it?"

"Where are these pictures now?" Jillian asked.

"In storage, at our Medford location. Thanks to our new computer system, everything is going digital these days. So, I heard my boss say they're planning on trying to contact the families the donations belonged to, but if they don't want them back, they're going to be destroyed."

I nodded. It made sense. My guess is that whoever donated that junk is not going to want it back. I mean, who'd want boxes of old photographs and papers when they existed digitally?

"I'll take anything that belonged to Dame Hilda Highland," Jillian suddenly said.

"What was that?" I asked, certain I had heard wrong. I

know my girlfriend. She was all about clearing out seldom used clutter.

"Zachary, look at this!"

I leaned over Jillian's shoulder and stared at the computer screen. There, on the display, was a series of pictures. It was Dame Highland, and it looked as though she was modeling her jewelry!

"Okay, she's wearing her jewelry in these pictures," I said, as I studied the thumbnails. "However, these aren't going to do us any good unless we find any of her other pieces."

"I'm talking about this picture. Look, Zachary! What does that look like to you?"

Jillian clicked on one of the thumbnails. A tiny picture suddenly expanded to fill the entire screen. It was a picture of Dame Highland, only it had to be a more recent photograph of her. All the other pictures I've seen had her in her teens and twenties. This one placed her in her late forties. But, all that aside, what drew my attention was what she was wearing. It was the necklace Jillian had found tucked away in that bookcase!

"This is it! This is proof! We have our provenance!"

Behind us, unbeknownst to either of us, one of the patrons calmly closed the book he had been pretending to read and pushed away from the small desk. He quickly gathered his things and all but sprinted for the exit.

TEN

You don't have to like it, Zack. What I'm saying is, the discovery of that necklace cements the fact our friend Mr. Stiller is going to be back. Soon. All I want to do is up the time table. Let's move on him before he can move on us. I think we can set a foolproof trap."

"How?" I demanded. "And using what? It's not going to be that necklace. It's safe and secure."

"He'll have a wide variety of choices to choose from," Vance assured me.

"Did *you* find Dame Highland's hidden treasure trove?" I suspiciously asked. "Otherwise, I don't know where you plan on getting any more jewels, unless you're planning on robbing a jewelry store."

"They're on their way over now, in the guise of a couple

of pizzas," Vance informed me.

"You didn't, did you?" I incredulously asked.

"What, rob a jewelry store? Come on, Zack. Be serious. And be on the lookout for those pizzas."

At the thought of a hot slice of pizza, my stomach rumbled. Loudly. "Sorry. That was me."

Jillian went sympathetic, "You poor dear. Are you hungry? We've been running around all day. I hadn't thought about getting anything to eat."

"I am hungry, but I have too many other things on my mind right now. Sitting comfortably at the top of that list is getting rid of our 'ghost'. I want him out of Highland House once and for all."

"You and me both," Jillian agreed.

I looked around the living room of Jillian's latest investment. She and I were sitting on the same couch we had found the clump of dirt under earlier. Vance was sitting in an armchair, only he hadn't bothered to pull the protective covering off.

"I have to tell you, buddy," I said, as I turned to my detective friend, "I'm a little nervous about setting a trap in here. Yes, we probably know we haven't seen the last of this Curtis fellow. Yes, he wants the jewelry. However, can't we lure him somewhere else?"

"Don't be a big baby," Vance teased. "Compared to what you and I have done in the past, this will be a piece of cake."

"I'm not comfortable with you sending a whole lot of jewelry here," I admitted. "Especially not in a pizza box. I mean, come on! What happens if the driver opens it up and looks in?"

"Please, Zack," Vance scoffed. "First off, the driver

will be a cop. And second, not one of the pieces will be real. They're all fakes, buddy. Every single one of them."

"How are fakes supposed to lure Curtis Stiller here?" I argued. "He'll take one look at them and know they won't be worth diddly squat. I'm pretty sure a professional thief will know the difference."

"What I'd like to know is," Jillian interrupted, "what are we supposed to do if Curtis discovers these are fakes and gets angry? What if he pulls a gun on us?"

"I'm glad you asked," Vance replied. He gave Jillian a grin. "My officers will be *everywhere*. You told me this house is full of hidden passageways and secret rooms, right? Well, we're going to make use of that. I'll have people hidden everywhere. That way, as soon as Mr. Stiller puts in an appearance, we'll have him. All we need for him to do is step inside. That's it."

"Far be it for me to rain on your parade," I hesitantly began, "but doesn't Curtis know all the secrets about this house? Wouldn't he know what to be looking for?"

"Possibly," Vance admitted, "but that's why we have to sweeten the pot. We have to make it look as though we've discovered where Dame Edna…"

"Hilda," Jillian corrected.

"…*Hilda* has hidden her stash. If that one necklace you found has a price tag over sixty thousand dollars, can you imagine what the rest of the collection must be worth today?"

"When do you plan on setting this up?" I curiously asked. "Not tonight, I hope."

Vance shook his head. "No, not today, but later tonight. We have a team who is planning on sneaking in here sometime after 2am to set everything up. As for when we'll spring the trap, that'll be tomorrow, late morning. It'll give us time to make sure we have all our bases covered."

I breathed a sigh of relief. Maybe I might be able to have a stress-free night after all. And, thanks to Vance and his suggestion of pizza, I was in the mood for a hot slice or two. Lost in my own thoughts as I busily assembled my future Italian delight, I didn't hear what Jillian said to Vance. But, his outburst, on the other hand, had me looking up.

"In the what?" I heard Vance exclaim. "Are you serious?"

"I am."

"Wait, what?" I asked, confused. "Who's serious about *what*?"

"I just told Vance where I found the necklace," Jillian explained.

"Have you two ever stopped to consider," Vance slowly began, "that more of the jewelry might be found hidden in other pieces of furniture?"

I smacked my head, just like the old V8 commercials.

"That's what we forgot to do. Of course! Thanks, pal. I knew I could count on you to point out the obvious."

Vance sighed heavily and turned to face me.

"Look, I'm sorry. I should've known the two of you would have already thought of that. What I'm trying to say is, since that necklace you found was hidden inside a piece of furniture, then obviously the furniture hasn't been that thoroughly checked. By Curtis, I mean."

"Okay, I can buy that," I decided.

"I mean, what if there was something hidden in this chair?" Vance wanted to know, referring to the arm chair he was sitting on.

I shrugged. "We still need to go through everything,

obviously. As for that chair, well, I looked under the tarp earlier. It's nothing but a basic-looking wooden chair you'd expect to find at a dinner table. Where would someone hide something on that?"

Vance wasn't to be deterred.

"Well, what about that couch?"

"What about it?" I asked.

"Could there be something hidden in that?"

"Again, it's possible, but I doubt it."

"Even though the dogs are staring at it as though there is," Vance continued.

I glanced down at the dogs. Sure enough, Sherlock and Watson were staring underneath it, as though they expected a mouse to come flying out at them. I fidgeted uncomfortably.

"That's where they found the clump of dirt," Jillian recalled. "There's probably a little bit left of it in the carpet. That must be what they smell."

Intrigued, I stared at the dogs. Watson looked up at me and whined. Then, Sherlock pawed at the couch. I let out a groan and slid off the couch, onto the ground, while Vance leaned back in his chair and flashed me a grin.

"Don't get your hopes up, pal," I warned him. "This is gonna turn out to be nothing. Ack! Guys, come on. Must you clean out my ears while I check out what's underneath here?"

Sherlock darted in and shoved his head under the couch, right next to mine. Watson wiggled her way into my embrace as I futilely tried to see if there was anything notable under the couch. I even pulled out my cell and activated the flashlight app.

"Anything?" Jillian asked.

"Nothing," I reported.

I sat back on my haunches and was ready to rejoin Jillian on the couch when Watson whined again. Both of the corgis hadn't budged, and Sherlock kept thrusting his nose under the couch every few seconds. *Something* was down there, but the question was, what?

I flashed back to the discovery of the tiny cube speaker we found up in the master bedroom. Could there be something attached *under* the couch? Maybe another speaker?

I handed the leashes to Jillian, who correctly guessed I was about to flip the couch over. She quickly rose to her feet.

"Vance, want to give me a hand here?"

"Sure."

Together, the two of us carefully rolled the couch onto its front, allowing us to study the undersides. The two of us inspected the couch itself while Jillian and the dogs headed to the space where the couch had been, just to see if there was anything concealed in the carpet. Both dogs, however, only had eyes for the couch.

"Zachary? Do you see this? The dogs are still staring at the couch."

"That cements it," Vance observed. "There's something up with this thing, but the question is, what?"

I poked a finger at the thin fabric backing of the couch. I could see that it had been attached using staples. I applied a little more pressure, causing the fabric to bow inward, but I still couldn't touch the couch's framework. That was odd, wasn't it?

I pulled my multi-tool from my belt. Being careful not to rip any of the fabric, I pulled nearly a dozen of the staples out, allowing us to peel back the black fabric. Still not able to see anything worth mentioning, I looked over at Watson, who was wiggling with anticipation. Inspiration struck.

"Hand me Watson's leash, would you?"

"Sure."

Jillian handed me the leash just as I bent down to pick the small red and white corgi up. Cradling her securely in my arms, I held Watson over several areas of the couch. Vance snorted with laughter.

"You're holding her like you would a metal detector," Vance observed. "Do you really think that's going to work? Oh, hang on. I think I want to film this. It's time I made you into a viral sensation on the Internet. I can just see the headlines now. Author uses dog to find missing jewelry! What a hoot that will…"

Vance trailed off as Watson let out a soft whine. We were directly over the far-left side of the couch. I held her over the center, nothing. Moving to the right, the small corgi was still silent. But, moving her back to the left? Watson whined again.

Setting the dog back on the ground, I removed another dozen or so staples. Peeling back the fabric from that corner of the couch, Vance suddenly whistled with surprise. Fastened to one of the wooden support beams of the couch, with thin metal bands, was a small tin canister, like something you'd find when purchasing a dozen cookies at Christmas.

Folding the blade back into my tool, and then pulling out the Philips head, I removed the brackets and caught the tin box as it fell loose. Rotating the tin container, I could see that it was advertising for some type of biscuit.

Also, as I rotated the tin, I could hear something thumping around inside.

"Oooo, Zachary, there's something in it!" Jillian exclaimed.

I passed the box over to her.

"This is your house, so you get to open it up."

She took the box, pried the lid off, and gently retrieved a felt-covered object. She moved to the nearest counter and slowly peeled away the coverings. She gasped out loud. Turning, she held up pair of glittering green earrings.

"Emerald earrings! Heavens above!"

"And *that* is why this trap is going to work," Vance crowed.

I looked up at my friend.

"And why's that?"

Vance pointed at the newly discovered earrings.

"Don't you get it? The missing jewelry? It's here, in the house! That crafty old dame hid it in plain sight. Dang, that's clever."

Jillian handed the jewelry over to Vance.

"Would you keep a hold of this for me? The bank has already closed, and I'd just as soon not take that back to my house."

"Seconded," I agreed.

Vance nodded. "Will do. Wrap that thing back up, would you? Thanks. I'll put it in my own safe tonight. I'm surprised, Jillian. I thought for certain you'd have a safe at your house."

"I have three, detective, but zero guns."

Vance thoughtfully nodded. "Gotcha."

"Would you explain to us how you are going to trap him?" Jillian wanted to know. "Are you at liberty to tell us?"

"Since I know the two of you won't be tattling to our perp anytime soon," Vance chortled, as he slid the earrings into an inside jacket pocket, "I feel it's safe to tell you. Okay, tomorrow morning, you, namely Jillian, are going to make a huge announcement. You're going to call the precinct and ask for armed protection, seeing how you just located a huge assortment of valuable jewelry."

"That's not too far off from the truth," I remarked. "Do you think Curtis has a police scanner?"

Vance shrugged. "I wouldn't put it past him. If I was him, I'd want to keep tabs on the local police department at all times."

"So, I pretend to find a huge cache of Dame Highland's jewelry," Jillian continued. "I then freak out, because I'm uncomfortable being around that much money, and call for police assistance? I shouldn't have any problems playing that part."

Vance nodded. "Exactly."

"When is this going to happen?" I asked.

"Let me confirm it with the captain. Just a moment."

"I can't wait for my turn," I softly muttered, as I watched Vance head toward the foyer and the front doors.

"Why?" Jillian asked.

"Because there are a few things he needs to clarify," I answered. "Namely, what to do if something goes wrong. Since I'm involved here, and I'm pretty sure Murphy's Law was written especially for me, I need to know what to do in case something doesn't go our way."

"It will go our way," Vance insisted, as he reappeared. He looked at Jillian and nodded encouragingly. "Ten a.m. The fun happens at ten. Does that work for you?"

"Of course. Vance, I do believe Zachary has a few

questions for you."

Shrugging, Vance turned to me, "Yes?"

"Since we're the bait," I began, trying my best to keep the frown from appearing on my face, "let's go over what we're going to do if and when something goes wrong."

"Like what?" Vance cheerfully asked.

Both Sherlock and Watson growled just then. Smiling encouragingly down at the dogs, I turned back to my friend and continued on.

"Oh, don't play innocent with me, pal. I know you've already thought this through. Help us, er, help *me* feel better. What's your contingency plan?"

"Okay, look, Zack," Vance said, as he lowered his voice, "you're right. I've thought through some scenarios that might happen. Bear in mind, I don't think they will, but Captain Nelson specifically asked about the same thing. He doesn't want to put civilians in harm's way."

"Well, someone is gonna get a Christmas gift from Lentari Cellars this year," I remarked. Jillian took my hand and squeezed it encouragingly.

Vance held out his hand and began ticking points off on his fingers.

"First, let's say Curtis Stiller somehow manages to get the drop on you. Think about it. He's here for one thing only: the jewelry. Give it to him. Trust me, he'll take it and run."

"And if he doesn't?" I countered. "What if he knows it's a fake and that he's been set up?"

"We've thought of that, too," Vance admitted. "Curtis has no idea if Hilda Highland's jewelry collection is 100 percent real. You could simply say that you thought the jewelry was real, too."

I grumbled, but I didn't say anything else.

"Okay, I have something that'll make you feel better," Vance said. He reached into a pocket and retrieved a small gray plastic device that was no bigger than a matchbook. To me, it resembled one of those clickers you'd use to train a dog. "Do you see this? It's a panic button. Press this, and a whole lot of boys in blue are going to appear, with guns drawn."

"Where will that be?" I wanted to know.

Vance shook his head. "Not only will each of you be carrying one of these, but there will also be no fewer than six of these things hidden around the house. Living room, kitchen, den, master bedroom, and a few bedrooms upstairs."

I had to admit, I liked that idea. And, I'm sure it showed on my face. Vance was smiling.

"Now, let's say Curtis appears and demands the real deal? That's assuming he's looked at the costume jewelry and knows it's fake right from the start."

At that exact moment, the doorbell rang. Both dogs lost their minds as they sprinted for the door, barking hysterically.

"No, I've got Watson," I said. "Vance, get Sherlock."

For the next thirty seconds, Jillian and I watched with amusement as Vance tried to snatch Sherlock's leash from the ground. Now, bear in mind, the leash was at least five feet long, so one would think that if you were unable to get your fingers hooked in the dog's collar, at the very least, you'd be able to grab the leash. Not in this case. Sherlock was literally that fast. Vance would stoop to snatch the leash, and Sherlock would dart away at Mach 3. Vance even resorted to trying to stamp his foot down on the leash, but

Sherlock was still faster. So, there he was, PVPD's finest detective, doing what looked like an angry tap dance.

You better believe I was recording it. I also managed to slip my phone back into my pocket by the time Jillian came to his rescue and, together, they caught the furry tri-colored missile. Grunting irritably, Vance handed Sherlock, who had been squirming in his grasp, over to Jillian. And, I'm proud to say that Sherlock stopped his antics the moment Jillian was holding him.

"Dogs," Vance grumbled, as he yanked open the door. "Hey, Jones. You're looking good, pal."

"Kiss ass, Samuelson," the cop irritably grumped, as the pizza boxes were thrust into Vance's hands. "Do you have any idea how itchy this outfit is?"

I had to look away to keep from laughing out loud. Officer Jones was wearing blue corduroy pants, a pastel orange polyester polo shirt, and a bright blue and orange paper hat. Vance, holding the pizza boxes in his left hand, reached into his pocket with his right.

"What are you doing?" Jones snapped.

"Don't you want a tip?" Vance managed to ask, between chuckles.

"Oh, shove it. I don't need … hey, not cool, bro! Put away the phone!"

Vance snapped a couple of pics and slipped his phone back into his pocket.

"This is going up on the precinct's Facebook page, buddy."

Jones angrily stomped away. Vance stepped back into the foyer, closed the door, and passed two of the pizza boxes over to me. A quick glance inside confirmed that they were filled with costume jewelry. Now, I have to say here that, if I hadn't been told it was fake, it would have made me look twice. I mean, I always thought costume jewelry looked the part, meaning it'd look obviously fake. This stuff? Wow. It looked real to me. I had to hand it to whoever made these things. They were getting really good.

But, it was still glass. My stomach didn't give a flying fig about glass. I wanted the box that Vance was holding.

"Cough it up, pal."

Vance grinned and handed the box over.

"Enjoy it, compliments of the PVPD. How much longer will you guys be here?"

"Not too much longer," Jillian assured him. "Once we finish up here, we'll straighten up, make sure everything is locked, and then head home."

"Sherlock and Watson haven't had their kibble yet," I added.

On cue, the dogs growled.

"Man, they're getting cranky," I said, as I eyed the dogs.

"You're going home together?" Vance wryly asked.

I sighed. "We drove here together, yes, but I'll be dropping her off at her place, you doof. Get your mind out of the gutter."

Vance laughed and headed out the door.

"Are you comfortable having dinner here or would you like to head to my place?" I asked, as I looked over at my girlfriend.

Jillian had already taken a slice of pizza out of the box and was in the process of taking her first bite when she paused. I grinned at her and then selected my own slice. Reaching into the accompanying bag of utensils, I pulled out two napkins and handed her one.

"It's not bad," I admitted, as I wiped the grease off my

face. "I haven't had a pepperoni pizza in a while."

"Me, either," Jillian admitted. "Whatever happened to a normal, *regular* pepperoni pizza? Why do they have to make everything so spicy?"

I shrugged. Spicy or bland, at this point, I was so hungry that they could have made this an everything pizza, and I would have eaten it, no questions asked. Also, I'd like to point out, for the record, that Jillian had also consumed several slices in silence. That tells me she was just as hungry as I was.

Both dogs shook their collars right then. A wave of guilt instantly washed over me. Here we were, feeding our faces, when the poor dogs were probably just as hungry as we are. Uh, *were*.

Before I could say, or do, anything, Jillian wiped her hands with her napkin and rose to her feet.

"We should probably get going. I have never liked eating in front of a hungry animal."

"You're referring to me or the dogs?" I chuckled.

Jillian swatted my arm, "You know what I mean."

I pointed at the two pizza boxes with the surprisingly realistic costume jewelry.

"What should we do with that? We probably need to hide it. I mean, what happens if Curtis manages to sneak by the police and get in here? If they see that, then Vance's trap is going to fall flat on its face tomorrow."

"We need to hide it," Jillian decided.

"Couldn't agree more, but where?"

"Would you put it back in the master bedroom closet?"

I rose to my feet and collected the boxes, "Sure. Umm, want me to put it in the hidden section? I mean, chances are, Curtis won't look there again. He's probably searched that closet from top to bottom several times by now."

"That's a good idea. Thank you, Zachary."

It only took me a few minutes to stash the boxes in a corner of the furthest reach of the closet's secret room. I ended up pulling a few outfits from their hangers and draping them over the boxes, concealing them from sight. Satisfied, I took a few steps back and smiled. If anyone would happen to discover this secret room, all they would see would be what looked like a pile of discarded clothes.

"Done," I announced, as I arrived at the bottom of the stairs.

I had expected Jillian to offer thanks, or at least make a noise, like she was rising from the couch. Instead, what I heard stopped me in my tracks.

"That's far enough, pal. Get your hands up, where I can see 'em."

There, standing in plain sight in the living room, was Curtis Stiller and an unknown second man. Curtis had a gun and was pointing it straight at Jillian and the dogs.

ELEVEN

Exiting the stairs and out onto the foyer, I could only stare, dumbfounded, at the two men. Curtis Stiller had an accomplice? Since when? And, who was he?

"I said, hands up!" Curtis barked.

Sherlock and Watson both growled at the intruders. Watson had her hackles raised, and Sherlock was baring his teeth. On a corgi, however, it just wasn't that intimidating. The problem was, no matter the age or the temperament, practically all Welsh Corgi Pembrokes looked as though they were smiling. Yes, Sherlock was baring his teeth, but there's no doubt about it: he just wasn't invoking any fear. Well, not much, anyway.

"Hush, you two. Look, pal, my hands are up, okay? There's no need for the gun."

"Agree to disagree," the second man sneered.

"And you are?" I politely inquired, as I turned my attention on the second man. For the record, I have no idea how I remained so calm addressing someone while a gun was pointed at us.

"If you don't know it by now," the second man snapped, "then I see no reason why you need to know."

Curtis nodded. "You tell 'im, Bart. Oh. Dammit."

"Dude, what the h——!" Bart exclaimed. "I always said you weren't the sharpest tool in the picnic basket, didn't I?"

"You did," Curtis sullenly admitted. He waved the gun at Jillian. "You. Princess. You're gonna tell us what you did with the loot. Where's the jewelry? Where have you hid it? I've searched high and low, but can't find no trace of it anywhere."

"That should be, 'what have I done', not 'what you did'," Jillian corrected, with a frown. "If you're going to threaten me, at least use proper grammar. Now, Curtis, you and Mr. Bart here are obviously looking for Dame Hilda Highland's missing jewelry, are you not?"

Both thieves nodded excitedly.

"Would it surprise you to learn that neither Zachary nor I have discovered it? We really don't care about the missing jewelry at all. The only thing I want to do is restore this house to its full glory."

"You're full of it, lady," Bart sneered. "I know good and well you found a necklace in here. Problem is, you got it out of here while Curtis had stepped out, even though he was under strict orders to watch you guys whenever you were here. Now, tell me, what have you done with it? It's ours!"

"Yours?" Jillian repeated, puzzled. "I'm sorry, are you

two actually descendants of Dame Highland?"

"Well, no," Curtis automatically answered.

Bart, being a few watts brighter than his cohort, nodded vigorously.

"Of course."

"One says no, and the other says yes," Jillian reported. "I do believe someone isn't telling the truth. If you want me to return the jewelry to the rightful owner, I would be more than happy to oblige. However, you have to prove to me you are a direct relative. So, can either of you do that?"

The two intruders looked at each other, as if each suspected the other might be withholding information.

"Ummm…" Curtis stammered.

"Listen, guys," I cut in. "It's clear you've been here a while. The two of you have been living in that second basement you dug below the first. How long did it take for you two to do that, anyway?"

"It was already there," Bart insisted. "We didn't dig anything. It was the perfect place to hide while we searched the house."

"How long have you been down there?" Jillian asked, genuinely curious.

"Long time," Curtis automatically answered. He gulped nervously as he noticed the dark glare his companion was giving him. "What? I didn't give her an exact time, did I?"

"It wouldn't be hard to figure out," I decided. "All you have to do is figure out when the reported ghost sightings started up. I'm sure if we check, then we'll see that more than likely, there was a time when the ghost was mysteriously absent."

"Eight months, all right?" Bart snapped. "We've lived here for eight miserable months."

"This time," Curtis softly added.

"What does that mean?" I asked. "*This time*? Holy crap. I get it now. You've been in this house before. Prior to your eight months. How long have you been coming to this house?"

"More time than I care to admit," Bart said, scowling. "That jewelry is rightfully ours. If you say you aren't interested in it, then give it to us now, and we'll be on our way. You can have this cursed house. That necklace you found? We want it back. We heard what you said about it. It's worth over sixty thousand dollars? That will pay off a lot of debt."

"But not all," Curtis whined. "Once we find the rest of it, all will be good."

"All of *what* will be good?" I wanted to know.

Both thugs fell silent.

"The necklace is upstairs," I said, after pretending to hesitate so I could consider their request.

"The only thing upstairs are those boxes full of fakes ," Bart sneered. "We already know what's inside. I gotta hand it to you, they look real. They just might have fooled us with it, so it's a good thing we've been here, watching you two, the whole time."

"We know all about the trap your cop friend is going to try and lay on us tomorrow," Curtis proudly added. "It ain't gonna work. We're way too smart to fall for that."

"At least one of us is," Bart softly muttered, under his breath.

"Besides, it don't matter," Curtis continued.

"It *doesn't* matter," Jillian sternly corrected.

"Fine. It doesn't matter," Curtis amended.

"Why doesn't it matter?" I asked.

"We'll be long gone by tomorrow morning," Curtis answered. "Ain't that right, Bart?"

His companion nodded. "Oh, that's the truth."

As God is my witness, I have no idea what prompted me to say the following sentence.

"Why in the world would you leave without the jewelry?" I innocently asked.

"The jewelry's already been found," Bart angrily snapped.

It had? This was news to me.

"Oh, yeah?" I curiously asked. "By who?"

"Whom," Jillian corrected, offering me a smile.

I shrugged. "Fine. What she said."

Curtis pointed at Jillian, "Her. You found it! I know you done found the goods, lady. Cough 'em up!"

"But I've only found one necklace!" Jillian insisted.

"You're lying!" Curtis accused

"You know we're not," I tried to calmly point out. "If what you guys say is true, then you know the insides of this house better than us. You've had more time to search. If there was anything else here, then logic would suggest you would have found it by now. Guys, there's nothing left to find. Besides, if we had found it, you would have seen us find it, right?"

"And that confirms it," Bart softly announced. "You found it. Curt said you did, but I didn't believe him. Now I do."

"Told you," Curtis grumped.

"Found what?" I wanted to know.

Bart held out a hand.

"The *Czarina's Tear*. We know you know what it is. We also know that you know how much it's worth. Where is it?

What have you done with it?"

"How many times do I have to say the same thing?" I demanded, growing angry. "We don't have any other stashes of jewelry hidden away anywhere. We haven't found anything besides that one blue necklace. You want me to be honest? Fine, I'll be honest. I want you two out of here. Completely. If I had the jewel, then I would give it to you. I don't want anyone to get hurt, and that's the truth."

"Where have you searched?" Jillian gently asked. "Maybe we can help you."

"Our family has searched everywhere," Curtis sadly reported. "For years."

"For years?" Jillian repeated, using a tone of voice which suggested she didn't believe him.

"Yeah, lady," Bart added. "Years. You have no idea what this place has done to our family."

"It's like a curse," Curtis whispered.

Overhearing, Bart nodded. "Exactly. First, it claims the life of my grandpa. Then, my father wastes his whole life trying to finish what Grandpa John started. He ran our finances into the ground. Do you get it? He ruined us, lady! I'm trying to restore my family's honor. Those jewels are going to right a lot of wrongs."

"A lot of wrongs," Jillian softly repeated. "Bart, about your grandfather. John, was it? You say he's been searching for the missing jewels, too? Dame Hilda Highland only died in 1947. You're not that much older than me. What possessed your father to dedicate his entire life to finding the Highland treasure?"

"That's a good way of phrasing it," I whispered to her.

"Shush. Let Bart speak."

Bart, however, fell silent. Jillian, waiting expectantly for an answer, turned her beautiful hazel eyes on Curtis. When both men began fidgeting uncomfortably, I suddenly put two and two together, and realized *how* these two men fit into the picture.

"You're descendants of the men who killed Dame Highland, aren't you?" I guessed, drawing a gasp from Jillian. "Your grandfather, John, was one of the men found dead the following week, wasn't he?"

A dark expression fell over Bart's face. He slowly nodded.

"My grandfather unwisely teamed up with some bum he recently met. Together, the two of them tried to get the old lady to cough up the location to her jewelry."

"Your grandfather tortured a poor woman to death!" I all but shouted. "And you two dare to come here to try and finish what he started? What the hell kind of men are you? You should be ashamed of yourselves!"

"My father blew all our money on this place," Bart snapped. Just then, he reached into the waistband of his pants and produced a pistol of his own. Thankfully, he simply held it in his hand without pointing it at anyone. "He shed his blood in this god-forsaken house. His obsession created a rift in our family. Finding those missing jewels once and for all will not only restore our family's finances, but will help me try and mend the fences with my family."

"Think you're nuts, do they?" I quipped.

I realize now that wasn't my smartest move of the night. All of a sudden, I was looking at the business end of a gun.

"What are you doing?" Jillian hissed. "Stop provoking them!"

"I can't help it," I whispered back. "It keeps coming out every time I open my mouth!"

"Then close it," Jillian pleaded. "For me!"

"Good advice," Bart agreed. The gun briefly swung over to Jillian before landing back on me. "Now, get up the stairs, both of you. Take the dogs with you."

I looked up the curving stairs and then back at Bart.

"Up the stairs?" I curiously asked. "Umm, why?"

"Just get movin'," Curtis snapped. "Come on. We ain't got all day."

"We don't *have* all day," Jillian corrected.

"What is it with you, lady?" Curtis grumped. "You're worse than my mother."

Back in the master bedroom, I could only turn to look at the two thieves with a skeptical look. What could they possibly want in here? Yes, there was a secret compartment in the closet, but they had admittedly already been through it. Yes, there was the large bas-relief sculpture stretching across most of the room's southern wall, but we had already investigated that, too. It was just as it appeared: a floor-to-ceiling fifteen-foot-wide sculpture depicting all manner of scenes. The room also had two large bay windows, but those had also been checked. What, then, could these two be doing back in here? Was there something we were missing?

Curtis gestured with his gun. He wanted the four of us against the southern wall. Once Jillian and I, each holding the leash to a dog, had our backs against the carving, Bart indicated he wanted us to move to the right. He then reached over to the bas-relief and pressed what looked like a small chest.

We heard a *click* and a small, 3-foot by 5-foot door

popped open. Curtis yanked the door all the way open and pointed at the darkened interior. Curious, I angled myself so I could see inside the hidden compartment. Like the secret room we found in the kitchen, this compartment was shallow, at no more than four feet deep. However, the compartment also stretched up, to more than six feet tall, and extended the entire length of the room from left to right. I guesstimated the chamber was around fifteen feet in length. Off the top of my head, I didn't know how much square footage that amounted to, but I did know it was the perfect place to hide valuables.

I eagerly slipped out my cell and hit the flashlight app. What I saw brought a groan of dismay from the two of us. This area, like the kitchen, had been well plundered.

"How long have you guys known about this one?" I asked, as I looked up at Bart. "I must confess, this is a new one on us."

"You didn't know about this one?" Bart incredulously demanded. "Please. We knew there was something here as soon as we saw that big-ass carving. What, do you think people typically have somethin' like that in their master bedrooms 'cause they like lookin' at it? It's clearly here to hide somethin'."

"He's got a point," Jillian admitted.

"Shush," I said, as I gave her a friendly nudge.

"What do you expect us to do now?" Jillian asked. "Neither of us have ever seen this. We just told you that we didn't know this was here."

"Ain't this the place where you found the necklace?" Bart asked, puzzled.

"No," I answered. "If the necklace had been in there, wouldn't you two have found it long ago?"

"He's got a point," Curtis said, with a snicker.

Bart's look shot daggers at his cousin.

"Where *did* you find it?" Curtis demanded.

"How is it that neither of you know?" I asked. "Bart, didn't you say Curtis' only job was to keep an eye on us? What was Curtis doing when you were away?"

Curtis punched me on the arm, "Zip it, buddy. You tryin' to get me in trouble?"

"Where *were* you?" Bart demanded, as he turned on his cousin. "You never said. Every time I asked, you changed the subject."

"It ain't important," Curtis insisted. "Let it go, bro."

Eyeing the two relatives, who in turn, were now glaring at each other, a thought occurred. If I could get these two into a full-blown fight, maybe we could escape during the ruckus?

"Bart, did you know that I wasn't even here when Jillian discovered the necklace? She was by herself. So, my question is, where was Curtis?"

"Shut your trap, fool!" Curtis hissed. His gun, which had been held limp in his hand, now swung around to center on me. "It ain't none of your business."

"But it's mine," Bart said. "Spill, cousin. Where were you?"

"I was hungry, all right? I'm tired of eating cold beans. I wanted hot food."

"Where did you go?"

Curtis mumbled something, but no one heard the answer.

"What was that? A little louder, dude."

"I went to Taco Bell, okay? I love their burritos."

"You say you're tired o' beans, but yet you ate a burrito?

Are you kiddin' me?"

Flecks of spittle flew out of Bart's mouth and landed on Curtis' cheek.

"Eww! Watch it, idiot! You spit on me!"

"Did not!"

"Did so!"

"How did these two ever make it by the cops?" I wondered aloud, as we watched the argument grow more and more heated.

"It was easy," Bart sneered, as he cast another dark look at his cousin. "Especially when there's more than one way to get in here."

"There's four," Curtis proudly answered.

"I know of only two," Jillian said. "Are there secret ways to get in and out of the house, too?"

"The old lady was a smuggler," Bart snapped. "She hid all kinds of things in her house. Do you know how many times she got raided? Five! Did the Feds ever find anything? Not once. So, of course there are other, more *discreet* ways to enter this place."

"Snuck right by him," Curtis crowed. "Never looked up."

Bart's gun was suddenly aimed once more at Jillian.

"Enough talk. You, lady, are gonna tell us what we want to know, or else we start pulling the trigger, get it? What more do we have to lose? Don't try my patience."

I held up both arms in the *I surrender* pose.

"Look, pal. Tell you what. Put the guns away. Let us find these jewels for you. If there's anyone in this town who can find loot that's been missing for years, then it's these two."

Both thieves looked down at the dogs, as if noticing

them for the first time. Bart snorted with disbelief, while Curtis was in the process of holding out a hand so he could pet Sherlock. A quick growl and baring of his teeth had the aforementioned hand yanked back, out of harm's way.

"Why should I trust you?" Bart demanded.

"You don't," I said. "And I'm not asking you to. You said it yourself earlier: if you take possession of the jewels, then you'll go. That's all I want you two to do. Leave. So, if that means I need to cooperate in order to make that happen, then so be it. Now, can we look around?"

"No funny business," Bart growled. "I got the gun. I give the orders."

"You *have* the gun," Jillian corrected.

"Stop doing that, lady!" Bart cried. "You're driving me nuts!"

Jillian handed me Watson's leash and I gave each of them a gentle tug. Once both corgis were looking at me, I offered them some slack in their leashes.

"Come on, you two. We have a job to do. We need to find some missing jewelry. Sherlock? Watson? If you ever wanted to impress me, now's the time to do it. Let's go find some loot, okay?"

Just like that, both dogs were on the move. I was led out of the master bedroom and down the stairs. Once we were in the foyer, the corgis led me back to the large game room adjacent to the den. Like the den and the servant's room, it had wall-to-wall paneling, so if there did happen to be another hidden room in here, then it was well concealed. I didn't see anything that appeared out of the ordinary.

Sherlock glanced back at me as he trotted through the open doorway, and then immediately turned left. Standing before the southwestern corner of the large room, I could only stare at my dogs with a skeptical expression on my face. There was something here? It sure didn't look like it. Sherlock, however, promptly sat, which was his way of saying, *I'm done giving clues, so the rest is up to you.*

"What is it?" I heard Jillian's voice ask.

Turning, I saw Bart and Curtis, standing uncomfortably close to Jillian. Shrugging, I stepped out of the way so that I could show them what was there, which was just an empty corner. Bart growled and clutched his gun tightly in his fist.

"There ain't nothin' there, bub," Bart told me, with a growl. "Try again."

I looked down at the dogs. Sherlock, who had been sitting on his rump as he stared at the blank corner, slid into a down position and refused to move. Watson joined him a few moments later.

"There's your answer," I told Bart. I pointed at the dogs. "You can see them for yourself. There's something here, otherwise they wouldn't have done that."

"But we've searched this room," Curtis protested. "Over and over. There ain't nothing in that corner!" Curtis caught sight of Jillian's disapproving frown and sighed. "There *isn't* nothing ... anything ... there isn't anything in that corner. Happy?"

Jillian nodded. "Yes, thank you."

I held the leashes out to her and, once she had taken them, approached the corner. I reached for my multi-tool on my belt, but that had the unfortunate effect of making both thieves flinch and grip their guns tighter. I held up my hands and showed them the tool.

"It's just a pair of folded-up pliers. Look, do you see this? I bend this, and then this, and lock them into position. Now, what does it look like?"

"Pliers," Curtis decided.

"Exactly. I'm unarmed. In fact, I hate guns."

"He really does," Jillian helpfully added.

I began by tapping the walls, hoping I'd be able to hear some type of tonal change should I encounter a concealed door. Nope. The movies make it look so easy, but it wasn't. Everything sounded alike to me.

Grunting irritably, I looked down at the dogs.

"Care to help me out, guys? You insist there's something here." I pointed at Bart and Curtis. "Right now, I'm with them. There's nothing here."

"Awwwoooooo!" Sherlock howled. He still refused to budge.

Jillian stepped up beside me and peered closely at the paneled wall.

"My eyes are better than yours. Maybe I can spot something you might have overlooked?"

I stepped back, out of the way, and waved my hand, "By all means, have at it. If I can't spot anything, and these two haven't spotted anything, and they've been searching for an extended amount of time, then…"

"Years," Bart grumbled.

"…I highly doubt that…"

"Found something," Jillian reported.

Both thugs were by her side in a flash.

"What is it? Whatcha find?" Curtis inquired.

"This piece of paneling is loose," Jillian said. She tapped an almost invisible seam between two pieces of panel. "I'd say someone has either pried this piece off the wall, or else it has somehow been moved."

"Get out of the way!" Bart cried, as he shoved Jillian to the side.

Sherlock let out a warning woof. Jillian patted the corgi's head and ruffled his fur.

"It's okay, pretty boy. I'm all right."

A loud crack made us jump. Even the dogs. Turning back to our hosts, we could see that Bart had managed to pry the paneling up and away from the wall. Curtis had wiggled his fingers under the seam and yanked, which resulted in breaking the panel in half.

"Hah!" Bart exclaimed. "I knew it! I just *knew* there was something here!"

Curtis glared at him, "No, you didn't. You had no clue, just like me."

With half of the wooden panel missing, we could all plainly see the beginnings of yet another hidden door. It took Bart less than ten seconds to frantically clear away the remaining bits of paneling. Once the door, in its entirety, had been uncovered, they both scrabbled furiously at the seam. Unfortunately, the seam was too narrow. The door had been fitted too snugly, and neither could find purchase to pry the door open.

Bart dropped to the ground, "Hurry! Curt, check over there. There must be some way to open this. Look for buttons, levers, anything!"

At this point, Sherlock finally moved. The tri-colored corgi's head swiveled, until he was looking at a nearby end table, which was resting against the wall nearly a dozen feet away. Curious as to what Sherlock was staring at, I walked over and studied the empty table. Then, I ran my fingers *under* the table, ignoring what felt like several fossilized wads of gum. And there it was. I felt a small, flattened, one-inch box that had a button on it. I cleared my throat and waited for the two goons to look my way.

"Step aside," I ordered.

Skeptical, Bart moved away. When Curtis made no attempt to move, Bart grabbed him by his arm and physically yanked him out of the way.

"Ow! Why'd you do that?"

"Just watch. Okay, do whatever you're gonna do, bro."

I pressed the button. There was a soft *click* and just like that, the newly discovered door was ajar. Letting out whoops of joy, both men pushed the door open and eagerly stepped through.

"How did they miss that door opener?" Jillian quietly asked.

Before I could answer, there was an exclamation of surprise. Then, Curt reappeared in the doorway, brandishing his gun. He pointed it at the two of us.

"You two. Get in here. We're not about to leave you unguarded. Now, go!"

I passed a leash over to Jillian without checking to see which dog it belonged to, and stepped through the doorway. Jillian followed close behind me. I slipped a hand into my pocket and pulled out my cell, since this would be a good time to use my handy-dandy flashlight app.

Once the LED had been activated, I was able to look around. We were standing in a very narrow tunnel which turned sharply left, and then angled steeply down. Was this a shortcut to the basement? However, after continuing down for what felt like several minutes, we reached the bottom. Bart was visible, and he was holding a tiny flashlight.

"I take it you've never been down here," I guessed.

Bart didn't bother acknowledging. He was too busy inspecting the small subterranean room we were in, clearly looking for loot. With all of us holding our lights above our heads, we could make out the size and shape of the tiny room. As we entered the small chamber, I ran my hands along the side of the wall. Concrete. This room must have been Dame Highland's secret vault!

It was roughly 12-feet by 12-feet, in the shape of a perfect square. A stack of crates was in the far corner. Several were lying open, their lids flung across the room. From my position near the center of the room, I could see that the crates contained bottles. Whiskey bottles. I shrugged. It made sense. Over on my right, I could see several long, narrow boxes stacked like books. Judging from the size, I guessed they were paintings. The wall opposite me had a row of four small pedestals, each of which were covered with cloths.

Trying to control my pounding heart, I lifted the cloth off the first pedestal. Underneath was a glass display case, which I was guessing to be about one-foot square. Sadly, the case was empty. I moved to the second. It, too, was empty.

"What do ya got there?" Bart called out. He hurried over so he could see for himself. "Did you open these? Did you take whatever was in there?"

"You can see by the dust that I haven't touched them," I said. I pointed at the two cloths that I had discarded onto the ground. "They were just like those other two. I was about to see what was under them."

"I'll take care of that, thank you very much. We don't need you trying to make off with the merchandise, do we?"

"I told you before, and I'll tell you again," I said, as I sighed. "I don't care about anything in here. I want you guys to get what you came for and then leave. Is that so hard to understand?"

"Even if there's a 500-carat gem in one of them cases?" Bart insisted.

"One of *those* cases," Jillian said, with an exasperated sigh.

"Whatever," Bart grumbled. "Think I didn't know about *Czarina's Tear*? What do you think kept us here for so long and kept bringing us back after we gave up?"

"We want that emerald," Curtis added, nodding. "It's ours, lady. And we're gonna get it."

"It's a garnet," Jillian informed them. "It's not an emerald. Yes, its green, but other gemstones come in green."

"So, you know about it, too," Bart accused. "I knew you were lyin', lady."

About ready to take an angry breath, Jillian laid her hand on mine.

"It's not worth it," she whispered. "Let them think whatever they want."

"Well, well," Bart gloated, as he whipped off the third cloth. "Lookee what we got here! Ain't that a sight for sore eyes?"

I caught a glimpse of something large and green in the case before Curtis eagerly crowded close and cut off my view. I should also point out it was about the size of a chicken egg. Did they find the demantoid garnet?

The next ten seconds slowed to a crawl. I saw Bart raise the butt of his gun, intent on smashing it down onto the case. Sherlock, who up until this time, had been resting at my feet, sprung up, barked once, and tore off. Watson was right on her packmate's tail. And, I should point out that both corgis were *sprinting* for the door, as though some type of predator was giving chase.

I've said it before, and I'll say it again. I trust my dogs. If they turn to leave the room, I'm bound to follow. However, if they *haul ass* out of the room, and I can see Bart was about ready to smash the gun down, then I'm guessing those two intelligent canines knew something that I didn't.

I snatched up Jillian's hand and bolted for the exit tunnel. I heard Curtis shout something at us, followed by a loud smash. Then I felt a searing pain hit my right shoulder, but I had no intentions of stopping.

That's when I felt the rumble.

Jillian and I made it through the doorway just as a heavy iron grate sprang up from the ground, effectively sealing the two thugs in the vault. A few seconds later, Curtis' face appeared on the other side of the bars.

"Hey! What'd you do? Open this up! Let us out of here or else I'll kill you all!"

I shooed the dogs up the tunnel while pulling Jillian behind me. We safely exited the tunnel and emerged into the large game room. I heard Jillian gasp with surprise as I suddenly felt woozy and started to stumble.

"Zachary! Oh, no! Hold on! I'm calling for an ambulance. Hold on!!"

Annnndddd … the world faded to black.

TWELVE

One month later, I was standing in the foyer of Highland House. The renovation was coming along nicely. The front entry had its mosaic tile floor refinished. The snooker table had been polished, re-felted (is that even a word?), and returned to the game room. And, much to Vance's chagrin, the balls were still pink. My girlfriend, it would seem, wanted to keep everything as original as possible.

I headed to the living room and took a seat. I was here to pick up Jillian and, together, we were going to head to dinner. As I leaned back in the chair, I felt another twinge of pain from my right shoulder. Well, it was bound to happen. After all, I *had* been shot.

Truthfully, it still haunted my dreams, but I wasn't

going to admit that to anyone. Not yet, anyway. And why wouldn't it? The simple act of moving my arm, currently in a sling, brings tears of pain to my eyes. Had the bullet hit either an inch or two in the wrong direction, I had been told, then I could've lost the use of my arm altogether. But, I'm told the wound could have been a lot worse.

Sure doesn't feel that way.

Anyway, I can't give you a firsthand experience on what had happened next because, much to my chagrin, I had passed out. Sure, I had been shot, and without realizing it, had lost a lot of blood. I do remember Jillian freaking out on me once we made it up and out of the subterranean cement room, but then that was it. The nice thing is, I know Jillian will never give me a hard time for passing out. Not like Vance would. Or did. But, I will say I think I earned a little more respect in my detective friend's eyes.

Ok, let's start with TweedleDee and TweedleDum. They, as you might have imagined, had been caught red-handed in the vault, as I have come to call it. Even handcuffed, as they were led away, the two cousins were threatening to lay into one another, as though they each believed the other was the reason why they had been captured.

As for us, we made it out of the vault before it sealed itself. How the dogs knew bad things were going to happen if that display case was damaged was beyond me. Who would have imagined that Dame Highland would have had a top notch security system installed on her vault in that day and age, *and* that it was still operational? And, somehow, the dogs knew they had to vacate the area, and do so rapidly. I really don't know why I still question the dogs' motives. They're clearly smarter than me *and* they know it. I'm just thankful no one else had been hurt.

Czarina's Tear had vanished. That's the official report. However, both Jillian and I knew what had really happened. Shards of green glass had been discovered on the ground inside the vault, so I can only assume someone had tripped and fallen on the gem. The fact that it broke clearly identifies it as being a fake. Too bad. I would have liked to have known what it had been worth.

Speaking of worth…

The fourth display case? It had remained covered, seeing how Curtis and Bart had more important things on their mind than discovering what else was waiting for them. No, it didn't contain the real *Czarina's Tear*. In my opinion, it contained something much better. It held the *Royal Danish* egg.

The *what*, you ask?

The *Royal Danish* egg was one of six missing Fabergé eggs belonging to the Russian Royal Family. This particular egg was delivered to the Dowager Empress Maria Feodorovna, born in Denmark as Princess Dagmar. She returned to Denmark for her father's 40th anniversary of his ascension to the throne. The egg had been a gift to commemorate the occasion. How do I know so much about this? Well, Jillian, for one, somehow recognized the egg almost immediately. I tell you, that is one well-educated woman. And second, that egg's value has been placed somewhere in the twenty to thirty million dollar range.

Yeah, you read that right.

Before you ask what we're going to do with the egg, I can tell you it has already been done. The egg has been returned to Russia. Well, it was given to the Russian Embassy in San Francisco, if you want to get technical. To say they were flabbergasted that a missing Fabergé egg had not only surfaced but was to be returned, no questions asked, was a serious understatement. They passed along their eternal thanks. I'm told the Russian government is trying to find some way to thank us, only I have no idea how.

Bear in mind, this happened while I was in the hospital, on some pretty powerful pain meds. I don't remember a thing about any of it. But, that's okay. I have no qualms about returning a stolen object to its rightful owner.

Work on Highland House was back on schedule. In fact, I do believe they're focusing on the kitchen today. If you're wondering about all the hidden rooms and compartments scattered throughout the house, I can pretty much tell you that everything has been indexed and catalogued. Well, what was left. I can't begin to fathom how many valuables Curtis and his partner must have stolen over the years. Or his family, for that matter. The contractors have strict orders to leave all hidden compartments and rooms exactly as they are. Jillian was serious when she said she wanted the entire house renovated. Every nook and cranny is being inspected to be certain it is safe. For the record, two more hidden rooms and five more hidden compartments had been found. Empty, of course, but I think it's still way cool.

Oh! I almost forgot to mention the jewelry. In order to address that topic, let me take you back two weeks, to the time I had finally stepped foot back inside Highland House after being shot.

Jillian had her hands full with the corgis. I had volunteered to take one of the leashes, but Jillian wouldn't hear of it. The last thing she wanted to see happen, she told me, was to have one of the dogs accidentally pull me off balance. And, since the corgis are strong little boogers,

I knew it was a possibility. Without the use of my right arm, or hand, I felt like a complete invalid, even though Jillian constantly reminded me I had another perfectly useful hand. Ever try to sign your name with your opposite hand? Yes, some can do it, but the vast majority of us can't. I would fall into the latter category.

"How are you doing?" Jillian asked again, concern evident in her voice. "I don't want you overtaxing yourself. If you get tired, you're to let me know, okay?"

"It's a promise," I said.

Let me cut in here again and tell you something. I really enjoy having an attractive woman fawn over me. I can definitely get used to it, especially when I actually needed the help. Again, not that I'd ever admit that.

"Do you think Dame Highland ever had the real *Czarina's Tear*?" I asked, as we headed to the living room.

Jillian nodded. "I do. I mean, think about it. Take that Fabergé egg, for example. It's Russian. It was stolen from the Russian Royal Family. What do you want to bet that egg, along with *Czarina's Tear*, were gifts from a prospective suitor?"

I shrugged, and then bit my tongue to keep myself from groaning aloud.

"Robert tells me they're going to begin repairing and replacing the wallpaper upstairs. The electrician will also be onsite, since he needs to identify … Zachary? What are the dogs doing?"

Sherlock had suddenly perked up, as though someone had blown a dog whistle. Watson had perked up, too, only she was a few seconds behind Sherlock. Together, the dogs rose to their feet and headed for the stairs. Detecting taut leashes, both dogs turned to look back, but not at me. They were watching Jillian, as if they knew *she* was the one to talk to when it came to the control of their leashes.

"Should we follow?" she asked.

I painfully rose to my feet, "Sure. We'd be fools not to see where the two of them take us, especially in this house."

The dogs led us up the stairs, slowly, as if they knew I had trouble keeping up, which I did. Jillian had given the dogs as much of the slack as she could, which afforded her the ability to follow me up the stairs. What she was going to do, if I lost balance, was beyond me. I had at least a hundred pounds on her.

"We're back in the master bedroom," Jillian observed, as we walked through the large double doors. "What's in here, guys? Is there something you need us to see?"

Sherlock and Watson walked straight over to the large bas-relief sculpture encompassing the entire eastern wall of the room and immediately sat. Curious, the two of us approached the large carving and then stared at each other. Sherlock turned his head just then, looked straight at me, and then woofed once. Then, the tri-colored corgi returned his attention to the huge piece of art.

"I'm not sure what we're looking for," I confessed. "Yes, this is a magnificent piece of work, but what the significance is, I don't know."

About ready to say something, Jillian's mouth suddenly closed. Curious, she edged closer and ran her hands along the many intricate details that had been incorporated into the sculpture. Her hand stopped and then her index finger started tapping.

"What is it?" I asked.

"Have you looked at this thing?" Jillian wanted to

know. "I mean, *really* looked? It's covered with carvings."

"I can see that."

"No, I mean, look at the carvings. This is a tower. If you look closer, you can see Rapunzel at the window, and strands of her hair have been let down, almost to the ground."

I nodded as I studied the scene, "That's pretty cool."

"And this here?" Jillian continued, as she moved to another scene. "This looks like it depicts a forest. See? There's a path running through the trees. And look! There's Little Red Riding Hood."

I nodded again, "Okay. I see that. So, it's full of nursery rhymes? Is that it?"

"Goldilocks and the Three Bears," Jillian reported, tapping a scene depicting the inside of a cottage and three bears seated at a table. "Here's a workshop with... are those shoes?"

"The Elves and the Shoemaker," I said. "I know the story."

"The Elves and the Shoemaker," Jillian repeated. "Zachary, the whole sculpture is filled with nothing but fairy tales."

I suddenly remembered Sherlock and Watson running free inside *Cookbook Nook* and where they had stopped, namely the Specialty Cakes section. If memory serves, Jillian had a picture hanging on the wall right beside the display.

"Specialty Cakes," I whispered.

"What was that?" Jillian asked. "What about it?"

"Your store. Your Specialty Cake section? Sherlock and Watson broke free and were found sitting in front of that section. Refresh my memory. Don't you have a picture hanging right next to that display?"

Jillian nodded. "I do, it's ... you're kidding! Are you serious? That picture is a scene from Hansel and Gretel!!"

"Another fairy tale," I said, as I looked down at the dogs. "And every time we come in here, the dogs are looking this way. Honey, what do you want to bet there's something else we need to discover within this carving?"

Jillian fell silent. Concerned, I looked her way. She was looking at me, almost as if I had started speaking tongues. Had I? Said something weird, that is?

"You called me 'honey'," Jillian said. She gave me a warm smile. "Michael called me that all the time."

"Oh. Uh, I'm sorry. I can…"

"No, don't you dare. Don't tell me you'll find something else to call me. I like it."

I smiled back, "You're on. Now, what do we need to do here?"

"Well, let's see. We have four fairy tales represented so far. Can we spot any others?"

"This looks like Aladdin's lamp," I said, as I pointed to an almost life-sized replica of the genie's lamp. "That belongs to the genie, right?"

Jillian nodded. "I believe so. Okay, we're up to five. Now, what about that castle? Whoever carved it did a fantastic job. There's so much detail! Why, it even looks as though one of the windows is a keyhole. How strange."

"Is that from a fairy tale?" I asked.

Jillian shook her head. "No, not that I'm aware of."

"There's a dragon over here," I said, as I tapped an area in the top right portion of the carving. "Weird. It has two heads."

"There's a sea on the left," Jillian reported, "and it looks like there's a pirate ship being attacked by a sea serpent. I don't know what fairy tale that's from, either."

We spent the next hour studying every square inch of the wall. Oddly enough, we couldn't identify any other fairy tales, only the five: Goldilocks, Red Riding Hood, Elves and the Shoemaker, Rapunzel, and Aladdin.

So, what does it all mean?

"I'm at a loss."

"I'm not sure what we need to do, either," Jillian admitted. "It's almost as if … Zachary! This piece moved!"

I hurried—as best as I could—over to her side. Jillian's hand was resting on the tiny hammer the Shoemaker was holding. Sure enough, I could see that it was gently pivoting in place, alternating from the 'ready-to-strike' position to the head resting on the tiny table. Bemused, Jillian left the hammer in the down position and tried a few of the other tools. They, too, pivoted in place. Eager to see what else was interactive, Jillian began poking and prodding the scene. When she pressed on the shoe the Shoemaker was holding, we were surprised to see it recess a fraction of an inch and emit a soft *click*.

"It's a button!" Jillian exclaimed. "Oh, how clever!"

"What is?" I wanted to know.

"This whole carving," Jillian explained, sweeping her arm across the fairy tale-themed bas-relief. "It's a giant puzzle!"

"Does anything else move?" I eagerly asked.

Jillian checked other various parts of the Shoemaker scene, but the tools were the only items that were able to be moved.

"Nothing else here. Let's try another scene."

Several minutes later, Jillian let out another exclamation

of surprise.

"The trees! Here, next to Red Riding Hood. These three, no, four trees can move! Not much, mind you, but just enough to signify … well, it could signify the trees swaying in the wind."

"Are any of them buttons?"

"No. Let me see. Oh! Look! Red's basket!" I then heard a soft click. "The basket is the button. How exciting!"

"Look for more!" I suggested. "There are three other scenes. There must be more buttons!"

I was right. The tip of Rapunzel's hair, resting just above the ground, swung gently to the left and right. Plus, several birds sitting on the windowsill next to Rapunzel could also be moved. This scene's button turned out to be the weather vane on the top of the tower.

As for Goldilocks, all three heads of the bears moved, as if they were going to look at each other. The button ended up being the head of the baby bear. As soon as Jillian pressed the fourth, we heard a louder *click* and just like that, all the buttons were back to their original positions.

"We have to hit them in the correct order," I guessed.

Jillian nodded. "I can get on board with that. But … wait. What about Aladdin?"

My eyes moved over to the carved representation of the lamp. Being the closest to it, I gently poked and prodded the wooden carving, but much to my chagrin, nothing moved. Not only that, there didn't seem to be anything else to Aladdin's scene beside the lamp. What that meant, I didn't know.

As I was studying the lamp, trying to ascertain its role in the puzzle, my writer's brain kicked in. These were fairy tales we're talking about. What if … what if the order of the buttons is the order in which the stories were published?

"Order of publication," I suddenly announced. "I think that's the order of the buttons."

Jillian nodded. "I'll buy that. Do you know when these were published?"

I pulled out my phone, "I will momentarily. Let's see. Aladdin and His Magic Lamp was published … wow. It was published before 1709. As for Rapunzel, well, Google says it was published around 1812. The Elves and the Shoemaker was 1806, and Little Red Riding Hood was 1695."

"You forgot Goldilocks," Jillian reminded me.

"Right. Sorry. Goldilocks … that was 1837."

Jillian turned back to the huge bas-relief.

"All right. If we drop Aladdin out of the picture, since there doesn't seem to be a button over there, then that would mean the oldest is Little Red Riding Hood." She pressed the basket. "Then, it'd be the Elves and the Shoemaker." The shoe was pressed. "Up next, we have Rapunzel." The weather vane clicked when pressed. "And finally, we have Goldilocks." The baby bear's head was pressed.

My mouth opened, intent on asking, "What now?" only before I could say anything, Aladdin's lamp popped free of the carving. I actually managed to catch it before it could fall to the floor.

"Nice reflexes!" Jillian praised.

I was about to hand the thing over when I noticed the lid of the lamp move. Curious, I lifted the lid and looked inside. Shocked senseless, I turned to Jillian and gently rotated the lamp.

Something large and heavy, wrapped in black felt, tumbled into my hand. I carefully unwrapped it and nearly dropped it when I saw what it contained. It was green, sparkly, and the size of a chicken egg: *Czarina's Tear*!

EPILOGUE

Y ou should've told me! Are you sure you want to do this? I mean, you could sell it and probably make a fortune off of this. Collectors love this kind of thing."

"Don't you, as well?" Jillian asked. "If I want to give this to you, then you can honor me by accepting."

I felt my face flush with embarrassment.

I guess I should explain. Nearly a week had gone by since discovering Dame Highland's hiding spot for the Tear. After placing a call to our newly adopted grandmother, Katherine, and spending a full hour on the phone with her as we gave her a recap of what had happened with her great aunt's house, Jillian and I decided to purchase a video conference device and make the return drive to Washington state. The facility where Katherine was living had the option to include wireless Internet in her room, but at a cost. We secretly took care of the first year's worth of fees and instructed the facility to bill us once the time had run out.

We demonstrated how the device worked by making a call to Hannah, one of Jillian's friends, who was standing by. Katherine was understandably delighted with her new toy, especially when she learned she had access to the Internet on the special *magic box*. We promised to check in with her every week, and also promised that we'd return for each and every birthday. I told Jillian that I was pretty certain we had done our good deed for the day. Anyway, seeing the old woman's face light up when she realized we would be remaining in contact with her made it worth the effort.

Thanks to another phone call several days after we returned, we found ourselves on yet another road trip, only we were heading south instead of north. This time, we were on our way to San Francisco.

The Consulate General of Russia had notified us and asked us to appear in person so that we could be personally thanked for returning a priceless treasure to the Russian people. While uncertain what the Russians had in store for us, Jillian decided to make the best of it by arranging a week long trip to the San Francisco area. She even made reservations at hotels which would allow dogs.

So, here we were, heading for San Francisco, only I wasn't driving my Jeep, and Jillian wasn't driving her Toyota Highlander. We were, instead, driving the car I had seen in many pictures in the last month or so. We were in Dame Highland's roadster: a 1930 Ruxton Sedan.

This automobile is a car enthusiast's delight. I'll be the

first to admit that I really wasn't a car lover, but this one would make a believer out of me. Where had it been located after all these years? Well, as it turns out, it was never really missing. In order to understand what had happened to it, I'd have to remind you how I mentioned just how much Hilda Highland enjoyed her car. She didn't just like it, she *loved* it. She took great pains in making sure her car was well cared for. Apparently, she sank so much money into her car's care that she created an ongoing agreement with the local garage. Once a month, the local garage would send a mechanic to Dame Highland's house and do a routine check-up. Repairs and replacement parts, regardless of the bill, would be taken care of by Dame Highland herself.

Knowing a routine like this would be expensive, and inevitably monotonous, Dame Highland deposited thousands of dollars into an account at the bank, to be accessed only by the mechanics. It was also written, in the contract she had drawn up with the garage, that, if for some reason, she was unable to keep the necessary funds in the bank to pay for the car's care, then the car's ownership would then pass to the garage *if* the car was kept in perfect working order.

When the garage took possession of the car for its monthly maintenance after Dame Highland was killed, they were unsure where to store the car, so they therefore kept the car in their spare garage. When a storage unit complex was built nearby almost twenty years later (yes, the same one Jillian was currently renting a unit from), the car was moved to an empty unit, and the funds in the bank paid for the storage fees.

Now, after all these years, the money in the bank was nearing depletion. The local garage, which changed names several times, but eventually settled on Rupert's Gas & Auto, should be familiar to everyone in Pomme Valley, seeing how it's the town's main gas station. That was why Mr. Rupert had been calling for Jillian. Since the Highland name had been a loyal customer for so many years, Vinnie Rupert, the present owner of the station, didn't feel comfortable taking ownership of the car. Therefore, once contact had been finally made, and Jillian realized she now owned a vintage automobile in what enthusiasts would call cherry condition, she selflessly gave the car to me. I hadn't realized I had made all those comments about Dame Highland's favorite mode of transportation, but Jillian had obviously remembered.

Later, it was discovered that Jillian had been right. Dame Highland had a steady stream of suitors, and one of them, a Russian by the name of … wow. I forget his name. Then again, it was a hard name to remember. It had a lot of vowels in it. Anyway, Count Whatshisname, rumored to be a distant relative of the Romanov family, must have absconded with the egg in an effort to win over Hilda's hand in marriage. We're guessing the *Tear* was also smuggled out of Russia at the same time, but since there's no documentation on its origins, Jillian became the rightful owner. At present, it was currently sitting in the vault of some bank in Portland, awaiting authentication from a certified gemologist, which I didn't even know was a profession.

Whatever.

Speaking of jewels, I should also mention, with regards to Dame Highland's missing collection, that it has been found. Kinda. Armed with the knowledge that Hilda had hidden the jewelry in plain sight, Jillian and I launched a thorough, systematic investigation of every single piece of furniture. Yes, it took a while, but … we found several more necklaces, countless bracelets and rings, and even a few tiaras hidden away in plain sight inside the house. Then, on a suggestion from me, we went to the storage unit and did the same to the furniture that had been removed from the house.

Two more necklaces, each more exquisite than the first, were discovered. A pair of sapphire earrings turned up in a previously explored—empty—credenza. Have we found all the pieces? I have no idea. Dame Highland didn't keep a running tab of what she had, and where she had hidden it. We'll simply keep searching. Who knows what secrets that mysterious house will turn up next? Only time will tell.

AUTHOR'S NOTE

I hope you enjoyed reading the story as much as I enjoyed taking you back to Pomme Valley. Each time we visit, I have to ask myself: what has changed? As with any town, things change. Businesses fold, others are created. Relationships falter, while new ones start up all the time. As for Zack, I'm gently, but assuredly, steering him toward a permanent path with Jillian. Will they ever get married?

As for Lentari Cellars, I still have to admit I don't care for wine. At all. But … I'm certainly learning a lot more about it. How to make it, how to nurture the vines, when to harvest, etc. Trust me, though. If you ever find yourself asking, wouldn't all this research into making wine make you want to try some? The answer to that is a definitive NO. :)

As for what's next, well, I have a brand- new fantasy,

with new characters, a new world, and a new type of magic in the works. It's taking a little time to properly develop, so I'll be starting that as soon as it's ready. Since NaNoWriMo (annual challenge in November, where authors try to write a 50K book in a month) is just around the corner, I've instead elected to write the next novel in my Corgi Case Files series. This time, Zack and Jillian are heading south, for some much needed relaxation. However, as is the case with many of us, even our best laid plans can hit a snag or two. In this case, it might be three or four.

Keep an eye on the blog. I've closed my CafePress account and have created a Zazzle account, which means be on the lookout for upcoming contests where you can win some merchandise! I'll even include some signed paperbacks.

Happy reading!

J.
October, 2019

What's next for Zack and the corgis?

It starts out as a fun road trip to Monterey, California, for Zack, Jillian and the two corgis, along with friends Harry and Julie. But when a dead SCUBA diver washes up on the beach where they are walking, well, the group feels a mystery unfolding.

Zack, Jillian, Sherlock and Watson, become embroiled in a race to discover what the diver had been doing when he died. Compounding their investigation is the presence of a group of playful otters, who just so happen to be using what appear to be gold coins as tools to open shellfish. Are the two events related? Could the deceased diver have located a sunken treasure ship off the coast of Monterey? Don't miss the *Case of the Ostentatious Otters!*

Sign up for Jeffrey's newsletter to get all the latest corgi news—Visit his website at AuthorJMPoole.com

The Corgi Case Files Series
Available in e-book and paperback

If you enjoy Epic Fantasy, check out Jeff's other series:
Pirates of Perz
Tales of Lentari
Bakkian Chronicles

Jeffrey M. Poole is a professional author living in sunny Phoenix, AZ, with his wife, Giliane, and their Welsh corgi, Kinsey. He is the best-selling author of fantasy series Bakkian Chronicles, Tales of Lentari, and the mystery series Corgi Case Files.

Jeffrey's interests include astronomy, archaeology, archery, scuba diving, collecting movies, and tinkering with any electronic gadget he can get his hands on. Fans can follow Jeffrey online at his blog: www.AuthorJMPoole.com